"MADAME HAS ARRIVED,"

the hotel clerk had said cryptically. Packard wondered just who "Madame" was, as he stood at his door listening to the faint stir of bedding inside. He knocked and waited and knocked again. Then the girl he had left at her own room an hour ago stood before him.

"Like it better here?" he asked flatly.

Packard's trained eye quickly scanned the room. His belongings had been disturbed—or had they been searched?

Packard felt the sudden stir of excitement as she looked up at him invitingly. It came in spite of his anger and distrust. It made him want her when he could not, must not want her.

PACKARD KNEW THE FIRST RULE FOR THE SECRET AGENT WAS TO AVOID PERSONAL INVOLVEMENT—ESPECIALLY WITH A BEAUTIFUL YOUNG WOMAN WHOSE ALLEGIANCE WAS IN DOUBT.

KNOCK

AND WAIT A WHILE

BY WILLIAM RAWLE WEEKS

WILDSIDE PRESS

It is when your spirit goes wandering upon the wind,

That you, alone and unguarded, commit a wrong unto others and therefore unto yourself.

And for that wrong committed must you knock and wait a while unheeded at the gate of the blessed.

The Prophet, KAHLIL GIBRAN

1

THE NERVOUS young lieutenant's wife in the silver fur jacket at last got herself together. She got her traveling case into her left hand, a brown fur coat over the same arm, her passport and health certificate into the right hand, and her glistening black handbag over that wrist. She smiled uneasily at the passengers waiting behind her and hurried away from the Frankfurt passport control counter toward the customs benches. Her husband waved from behind the glass door, and the line of people in back of her moved ahead and Packard Gray put his passport on the counter in front of one of the men wearing the German green uniform and high-peaked cap.

The German took his American passport without looking up.

"You are with the Occupation?" he asked.

"No," Packard said.

"Your currency form?"

He held out his hand for the form but he did not look up. With his other hand he began to turn the pages of Packard's passport.

Packard unfolded the large currency sheet that he took out of his pocket. He laid it on the counter and the official had to move his eyes and his hand to pick it up. He looked at Packard with annoyance. Packard smiled slowly at him and then stared across the room.

Other officials in green uniforms moved behind the low metal top of the customs counter, waiting for baggage handlers to put the suitcases in front of their owners. A yellow tractor rolled up a ramp and into sight outside the building, pulling behind it two flat trailers piled high with bags. Doors in front of it opened automatically and it rolled into the room.

While the doors stayed open Packard looked out across the airport, dark and cold and windswept. It was just past three in the late November afternoon, but already lights burned across the field on the Air Force side. A gas crew stood on the wing of a Swiss Air DC-3, coat collars turned up against the short, biting snow flurries. The number one engine of a KLM DC-6 behind it coughed up a cloud of black oil smoke and a thumb of flame then steadied. The man standing under the engine exhaust with a fire extinguisher wheeled and trotted out of the way.

The outside doors swung shut. Across the customs shed

1

outbound passengers in the waiting room sat and read or sipped cognac for preflight courage. Some of them stared idly into glass cases of last-chance bargains like cameras and watches and dolls in gold and red native costumes. The hard double thump of the passport stamp brought Packard's eyes back to the official before him.

The man had closed the passport and held it out. He looked closely at Packard.

"You have come directly from New York?"

"That's right."

"You will please see the sergeant."

He laid the passport down on the counter for Packard to pick up. He motioned with his head toward a desk at one side of the room where an American master sergeant sat. A sign told all American civilian and military members of the Occupation Forces to present themselves to the sergeant.

"I am not in the Occupation," Packard said quietly.

The German glanced at a piece of paper in front of him. Packard could see the same kind of paper in front of each of the other inspectors.

"Nevertheless," the German said, "we do not make a mistake. You will please go to the sergeant."

Packard put his passport into the breast pocket of his sports coat and went to the desk. The sergeant looked up from his paper work.

"Can I help you, sir?"

"Hello, Sergeant; I was asked to come here."

"Your passport, sir."

The sergeant held out his hand for the green book. He put it in front of him on the desk and began to turn the pages.

"In the Occupation, sir?"

Part of Packard's mind was amused. If you are an American in Germany you are probably some part of the Occupation. Placement by position. Identification by geographical location. It could be a broad new theory, and it was good and important for him to remember it.

But another part of his mind was not amused. This was the part that did not relax. What small sense of humor it had was macabre. This part listened for the echoes after each sound. It felt ahead for the soft spot that meant a trap in the path. It looked backward into the blackness beyond the lighter shadows. It kept Packard Gray alive and he took even its routine warnings very seriously. Now it was stirring. If gently.

As much as it annoyed him, as tired as he was of doing it, Packard grudgingly went through a check list because of its stirring. On the ground in Frankfurt twenty-five min-

2

utes and they had asked him about the Occupation twice. Two curious or too casual? No. Routine. Identification by geographical location.

Had his answers drawn special attention? Negative. The German hadn't looked up. Nor the sergeant.

Still he was at an MP desk reserved for members of the Allied Occupation. Why had he been moved out of the normal pattern? Because of the white slips before the German officials. How did his name come to be on such a paper? Unknown. What about his person or effects?

Packard leaned on the MP counter with his left elbow, his chin in his hand, and glanced down at the passport.

New. Scrupulously checked. Normal. In order.

Clothes? Brown loafer shoes. Not new. Dark brown worsted slacks. Not new. Lighter brown sports coat. Not new. Reversible topcoat. Tweed on one side. Gabardine on the other. Old. Howland's book, *Germany and Hitler*, under his arm. No hat; no gray flannel slacks; no dispatch case; no trench coat. No usual trade marks of the American government employee overseas. Only his crew-cut hair. To make him look younger.

Luggage? Packard watched the baggage handlers. They dropped the cases heavily onto the metal platform and added sharp slapping noises to the hollow booming of the room. The German customs officers listlessly asked a question of waiting passengers and scrawled a chalk clearance on leather or cardboard before the question was answered. If the subject was not American or German, Customs as listlessly gave an order and dutifully pawed through the exposed contents of a bag.

Had ground crew or handlers had time to check through a suitcase? No. And if they had? Nothing. Packard was a professional.

What else? A leak in Washington. Ten thousand to one against a leak from Special Assignments. And if there had been, the Germans would have watched or followed or waited. They would not have alerted him.

He had it then. And he shook his head slightly because the move would not be clumsy and not quite clean. But he relaxed against the counter, and that one part of his mind settled to its uneasy rest, satisfied.

"Has your baggage come in yet, sir?" the sergeant asked.

He had finished with the passport, but he did not offer it to Packard.

Packard nodded.

The sergeant looked steadily at the papers in front of him. "You have anything to declare?"

"No," Packard said, and saw the way it would work.

3

The sergeant slid his forms into a drawer and locked it. He took his hat off the shelf beside him and put it on. He stood up in his military capacity. He did not say sir.

"Will you come with me?"

Packard said, "Sure."

He said it with surprise.

"Anything wrong?"

"Just come with me, please."

They walked together until Packard found one of his two suitcases and stopped before it. The sergeant put one hand on the low platform and vaulted to the official side.

"Very graceful," said the man who stood beside Packard.

Packard turned his head to look at him. He was big and fleshy and probably tall, but his weight made it hard to tell. His light brown suit was double breasted, its material created by science for a wrinkle-free Atlantic flight. It was expensively tailored but sleek. His head was large, narrow at the top, wide across the fat of his jowls. The eyes, nose and mouth all seemed to be recessed into the mass of it. His mouth was loose below a gray, trimmed mustache, and his hair was turning gray. His eyes were small. The whole face looked pompous and indulged and ready to be petulant or violent or ready to make love. He was smoking a cigar which he delicately kept from getting soggy. He had his dark overcoat folded over his arm as if it were not cold.

The sergeant looked hard at him because he had heard the remark. But the man appeared not to notice him, and the sergeant looked down and tapped the brown suitcase in front of Packard. It was old, scratched and many labels from many hotels had been peeled from its sides.

"This yours?" he asked Packard.

"Yes."

"Open it for me, please."

Packard pulled the cracked leather straps through the buckles; he pushed the spring latch. He held the well-packed contents in place carefully and spread the open case in front of the sergeant. The soldier pulled out two cartons of Pall Mall cigarettes and a fifth of good Jameson's whiskey that Packard had bought in Shannon. He was not loud, but when he spoke passengers looked down the counter toward him.

"Any other bags?" he asked.

"One more," Packard said.

He saw it down the line, beyond the man with the cigar. "There it is."

The sergeant motioned to a customs man who shouted at a bag handler who put down the luggage he was carrying and brought the case.

"What is this?" Packard asked. "What's the matter? I

4

don't even have all the cigarettes and liquor I am allowed."

He looked at the sergeant anxiously. His voice was worried. He would try to help them.

"Sure," the sergeant said. "This other bag is pretty heavy."

"I can open it for you," Packard said.

"Never mind. You'd better bring both bags and come with me."

"Now wait a minute," Packard said. "I haven't got anything I shouldn't have."

"Haven't you?"

"No."

"Then you don't have to worry. Come on."

Packard thought it was enough. He stood quietly and looked at the counter with embarrassment and concern. The sergeant picked up the two cartons of cigarettes and the bottle of whiskey and dropped them into the open bag. He started to slam the two halves of it together. Packard stopped him with his voice.

"That won't be very neat."

"No?" the sergeant looked up.

"No."

"O.K. You take care of it."

He stepped back and put his hands on his hips.

"Thanks," Packard said.

He began to close the grip.

The man in creaseless brown watched Packard through a thin line of smoke coming off the ash of his cigar.

"Trouble?"

"I don't think so," Packard said. "I hope not. I think everything will be all right. I don't have anything I shouldn't."

He didn't sound sure, but he smiled.

"That doesn't matter," the man said. "Military justice is a very democratic process."

"You take care of yourself, Mac," the sergeant said. He was rocking on his feet.

"I'm not part of your army," the man said.

"Are you an American?"

"I am."

"Okay then. In this part of Germany you're in the American Zone and under the responsibility of the American Army. See you remember it."

"I can see that I won't be permitted to forget it."

Packard didn't want the attention or the interruption that this exchange was bringing.

"I'm not in the army either." It was an effort to make peace.

5

"Then don't go with him." The man pointed the lighted end of his cigar at the sergeant.

"You heard what he said."

"Well, I wouldn't go." He waved his cigar as though to dismiss the sergeant.

"I'll bet he thinks you would."

Packard pulled the second buckle tight. He lifted both suitcases easily and waited. The sergeant looked hard again at the man in brown and walked away. Packard kept pace on his side of the platform. When the sergeant came to the narrow passage through the counter he turned and led Packard to a door. On the frosted glass is said: AMERICAN MILITARY POLICE.

The sergeant opened the door and walked in first. Packard turned sidewise with his luggage and followed him into the small room.

2

AGAINST THE far wall was a plain desk of light oak with two telephones on its top. There was a wooden swivel chair with arms behind the desk and a straight-backed wooden chair beside it on the left. On the right wall was a picture of President Eisenhower in uniform behind a cheap glass frame. Behind the open door so that it could be seen from outside the room was another yellow oak armchair from Army Quartermaster stocks.

The small man sitting in it wore a heavy, shapeless brown tweed suit. He had his left elbow on the arm of the chair and held the short end of a smoking cigarette between first and second fingers that were stained a brown as dark as his suit. He was nearly bald.

The sergeant closed the door behind Packard and held out the passport toward the corner.

"This is Gray, sir," he said. "I opened one suitcase. There was only two cartons of cigarettes and one bottle of Irish whiskey. The rest must be in the other one."

The civilian let the cigarette drop on the floor and stood up.

"Thank you, Sergeant, I'll take care of Mr. Gray. You can go back to your desk."

"Well," the sergeant said, "I'm supposed to wait around if there's a search. Just in case there's a gripe. There has to be a witness."

"I know. But Mr. Gray does not look to me as one who will gripe. I take the responsibility."

6

"The regulations, sir, say I should stay."

"Major Robbins told me to handle this case, Sergeant. Would you like to call him?"

"Not if you say so, sir. I just don't want to stick my neck out. "I'll wait outside."

When he left, the man held out a small hand.

"It's a good thing he didn't call," he said with a sly pride. "My name is, eh, Mayer, Mr. Gray."

Packard shook hands. He made a guess from accent and appearance. The man had originated in Central Europe. Austria. Perhaps Hungary. Or Germany.

Packard stood waiting beside the door, his hands stuffed in his overcoat pockets, the book under his arm. Mr. Mayer walked past Packard and sat in the swivel chair behind the desk. He looked at Packard's passport. He pointed to the straight chair.

"Sit down, please, Mr. Gray. We have only the few minutes that I should be looking in your suitcase."

He threw the passport across the desk to Packard.

"I know who you are," he began to recite abruptly. "You are Packard Gray. You come to Germany as a student to enroll in the University of Munich, where you will do advanced study in German history. But your actual study will be of those movements which are trying to prepare Germany for another Hitler. The University will be your cover. That's all right, isn't it?"

Mr. Mayer lit another cigarette for himself, then offered the pack. Packard shook his head. He frowned at all of the deliberate theatrics of the introduction. And its professional bad manners.

"You seem to know a lot," he said, "and to be anxious to tell it."

Mr. Mayer looked at him, displeased.

"I know why you are here. I know that you work for . . ."

"Mr., eh, Mayer," Packard interrupted before he could say the words, "will you get it done? I have a train to Munich to catch."

Mr. Mayer leaned toward Packard.

"You do not have to fear if I say names here, Mr. Gray; I have checked this room for myself. It is not wired. There is no office next to it. But I am glad to see you are careful."

"Good for you," Packard said.

Mr. Mayer ignored the comment. "I know that you are a friend of Nick's, then," he said. "I am a friend of his too, and in the same way."

Packard knew Nick. It was a pseudonym of the Chief of OSA. The Office of Special Assignments. His organization.

7

"Does the Nick you know have a business phone?" Packard asked.

"His home phone is zero, zero, seven, zero."

It was the seal. Each foreign agent of OSA carried the formula for identification. Packard sat back in his chair.

With a backhand flip, Mr. Mayer threw the stump of his cigarette, still burning, onto the floor.

"The German pass control was asked to send you to the sergeant to get a message. The sergeant was told that you might be engaged in smuggling. Not a capital offense. Quite."

"I understood it," Packard said dryly.

"Well," Mr. Mayer said. "Congratulations. All of this was done so that I could talk to you without attracting attention."

"But it did attract attention."

"So that it would not attract dangerous or embarrassing attention."

"Any attention embarrasses me," Packard said. "I have the academic point of view, Mr. eh, Mayer. Withdrawn. I could have been visited at leisure in Munich."

"I have been told of your withdrawn disposition," Mr. Mayer said. "That you withdrew into Yugoslavia for OSS by parachute during the war. That you withdrew from the Indo-China coast not so long ago by submarine. For one of your age you have done a great deal. But you should know that I also am not inexperienced. I have been a professional in these activities for a very long time, almost since my childhood in Buda. Where they were necessary for me to stay alive."

"Ah," Packard said, "one of the Old Professionals."

"I brought you here this way because there was not another method. I could not wait; I did not dare miss you; and I wished to see you in privacy."

Mayer got up and came around the desk and stood over Packard.

"You are not to go to Munich. Today is Monday. You will go directly tonight to Cologne and take the bus to Bonn. Tuesday, tomorrow, at half past two in the afternoon you will take the Sabena passenger helicopter service to Brussels. You have already a reservation which you will pick up at the Sabena office tomorrow morning. There is a reservation for you tonight at the Rheim-Palast Hotel in Bonn."

"Unfortunately," Packard said, "my itinerary was planned in detail by Washington before I left."

"I have been asked by Nick to tell you that you will spend the two weeks before your studies begin in a tour of the Low Countries," Mr. Mayer said.

"I had planned to spend that time looking for a good

8

tutor and a place to live," Packard said. "Do you have a note from Nick with you?"

"I do not."

"No, of course," Packard said. "An experienced man would not carry it around. Still, I would like to see the instructions. You do understand?"

"I do, but I should think . . ."

"Of course Nick would recognize the name, eh, Mayer, if he should hear it?"

The small man answered without embarrassment.

"No," he said. "It was thoughtless that I used a name that he would not know. Nick would know Stern."

"Thanks," Packard said. "If I go on to Brussels, what do you recommend there?"

"I have made a reservation for you Tuesday night at the Cosmopolite. On the Place Rogier. Not far from the heliport. You will enjoy an apéritif tomorrow at the Roi d'Espagne in the Grand' Place. You will easily recognize the bar. Dead pirates hang from the ceiling. A stuffed horse stands by the staircase. A fireplace fills the whole center of the room—often with smoke."

"What is the best time?" Packard asked.

"I would say exactly at six. That is before the real crowd and yet the bar will not be empty. You can dress just as you are. But perhaps you have a necktie? You might wear it. A red one? Well, it makes no difference. And take with you your book."

Mr. Mayer took a black loose-leaf notebook from his coat pocket, and a pencil. He made some notes and copied the title of Packard's book on one page. On another he wrote a number.

"I will know where to reach you today and tomorrow," he said. "After that you can check for telegrams or mail signed by Lois at the American Express Company in whatever cities you visit."

Mr. Mayer sat on the edge of the desk. His toes scarcely touched the floor.

"I do not know what those cities may be," he added. His tone implied that he regretted this loophole in his knowledge.

He handed the notebook page to Packard.

"If there is great need, you can leave a message for me, Mayer, at this number. It is a Frankfurt civilian number."

Mr. Mayer took a single cigarette from an inside pocket and lit it.

"Since you will not wish to drink alone," he continued, "a friend of ours named John will join you. John smokes a pipe and he will not light it with anything but an American kitchen match. He will speak of the time he saw Nick in

9

Belgrade, and he will contact you first. In the event that this meeting does not occur, you will be the next morning at eight in the dining room of the Palace Hotel. Please dress the same and carry your book to the table."

Mr. Mayer motioned toward the door. Packard stood up and studied the telephone number on the sheet of paper. He handed the page back. Mr. Mayer brushed a loose pile of cigarette ashes from his coat with the back of his hand.

"Have you been in this part of Europe before?" he asked.

"I was in France and southern Germany at the end of the war."

"Then you have some languages?"

"Enough."

"It always surprises me to find a native American who does."

"Well," Packard said, "I'll get in touch with Nicolas."

"It isn't necessary. But if you prefer it . . . "

"I do."

Packard picked up his suitcases. Mr. Mayer stood ready to open the door.

"There is one more thing," he said. "On the helicopter to Brussels there will be a quite famous young American lady . . . Miss Sarah Borsen. You know of her?"

"The reporter?"

Mr. Mayer nodded.

"It is because of her that you are to go to Brussels on the helicopter. We hope that you will become a good friend of hers on this trip. It will be less hard because she is very attractive as a woman."

"I see," Packard said. "That isn't much time."

"You are right, Mr. Gray. There is not much time. Uh, you will remember the names and places without trouble?"

"Yes," Packard said, "I will remember."

Mr. Mayer was lighting another cigarette. His last one was smoking on the floor close to one of Packard's grips.

"Would you please say them to me? Once?"

"Rhein-Palast Hotel, Bonn, tonight," Packard said. "Sabena helicopter to Brussels tomorrow, Tuesday, at 1430. Brussels, Cosmopolite Hotel. Drinks tomorrow, 1800, Roi d'Espagne. John; pipe; kitchen matches; knew Nick in Belgrade. Alternate: Palace dining room, 8 A.M., Wednesday. Miss Borsen, Sarah, make advances to. Beyond Brussels check American Express for word from Lois. Your telephone: Mayer, Frankfurt Civilian Exchange . . ."

"Yes; thank you; that is all of it."

Mr. Mayer opened the door so that he was behind it. As he squeezed out, Packard could hear Mr. Mayer's voice loud and clear.

". . . such a mistake," it went. "We hope you will understand the problem, though, and forgive us."

The voice had no accent.

Packard walked back across the customs benches. He saw the sergeant go into the Military Police room. Almost immediately he came out to join Packard.

"Okay, Herman," he said to the customs officer who immediately scrawled a chalk release on the top of both bags.

"I'm sorry, sir," he said to Packard. "But we have to check every tip that somebody gives us. I hope it's all right now. Will you take the airport bus to town? It's leaving right now?"

"No. Everything is fine, Sergeant," Packard said. "Where can I change some money and send a telegram?"

The sergeant pointed to the glass doors at the far end of the platforms.

"Go through those doors, sir, across the little lobby, through the outside doors and turn right. Then go into the big main entrance and you'll see signs. All the offices are in there."

"Thanks." Packard picked up his suitcases and walked away.

The angry man in brown was waiting in front of the KLM ticket booth when Packard walked in through the main entrance. He saw Packard at once.

"Well you aren't in jail anyway," he called.

Packard noticed faces turn to stare.

"No; not this time."

The man stepped away from the ticket counter to intercept him. "What was the matter?"

"Nothing. They thought I was carrying something illegal."

"Were you?"

"No."

"Very fortunate. That soldier was out to make trouble. Did you hear how he spoke to me?"

"You weren't very polite to him, either."

"Wasn't I? Perhaps that is because I pay taxes that pay his salary, and I expect respect. We have our own country filled with policemen and investigators, and we're filling up Europe. I don't care for any of them. Do you work for the government, too?"

"No," Packard said; "I'm here as a student."

He squinted his small eyes and studied Packard. "A student? You look old for that."

"I feel fine."

The man tipped an ash from his cigar neatly, with one blow of his forefinger, and went on with his observations.

"No wonder everyone hates us. They can see how we're taking over. They fear us."

"Do they hate us? I just got here."

"Well, I know they do. I'm a publisher and I talk to the people. Big and small."

"I see." Packard put his bags on the floor.

"I come to Europe three or four times a year on business and I know the place. They may hate our country. But, no one has ever said, 'Go home Farrel' to me."

"That's fine," Packard said. "If you'll excuse me, Mr. Farrel, I have to hurry."

"You're going beyond Frankfurt?"

"Yes."

"Where?"

"Cologne first, I think."

"Oh, Köln," Farrel said, rounding his thick lips for the German pronunciation. "And then?"

Farrel's questions were more than politely curious. It was becoming an interrogation.

"I don't know that," Packard said shortly.

Farrel plugged away at it. "Are you going to study there?"

"I'm always studying."

"I see."

Farrel turned back to the KLM counter where a blond girl in a blue uniform had been waiting for him with an official smile. She was holding on to a ticket envelope while she listened to him. Packard saw Farrel's suitcases on the scale below the counter.

"Well," Farrel said to Packard, but for the benefit of the girl, "take KLM. You get service on a European line. And their young ladies are always anxious to please."

He leaned on the counter toward the girl and smiled. He kept his still neat cigar at a considerate distance.

"Isn't that right, miss?"

"I'll keep what you say in mind," Packard said.

He lifted his suitcases and walked past the world map on the wall and the rows of new airline counters to the information booth in the next room.

"Why, no," the prim lady attendant told him in British English. "There is not a flight to Cologne this afternoon, but there will be a bus directly to the Frankfurt station in twenty minutes, and the trains are frequent."

Packard changed a twenty-dollar traveler's check into German marks, and he wrote out a wire to Mrs. P. S. Gray, who did not exist, at an address in Washington which did not exist: WILL SPEND NEXT TWO WEEKS LOW COUNTRIES ON INVITATION OF STAR WIRE ANY OBJECTIONS IMMEDIATELY HOTEL COSMOPOLITE BRUSSELS LOVING PACKIE.

He read it over. Stern was German for star. It gave the name some protection without being obscure or cute. His own signature was, unfortunately, as it had to be to be accepted as authentic.

Packard sent off the wire. He looked at his watch and walked back through the lobby and sat down at a small table in the waiting room for outbound domestic flights, and ordered a beer.

He pushed the wire spring off the porcelain top of the green bottle the waiter brought and poured the dark, heavy beer into his glass. People moved aimlessly around him with preflight nervousness. An American Artillery lieutenant who did not seem to have a wife sat on a couch across from him with a baby in his arms. Another girl of about three in a pink dress sat beside him quietly looking at a doll.

A round, red German woman at the next table rocked back and forth on her chair with loud laughter while her husband looked on pleased. Packard raised his eyes to the glass souvenir counter that separated the foreign and domestic waiting rooms.

There was a twin-engined KLM Convair on the ramp outside the foreign waiting room. Farrel paced impatiently back and forth before the red cord that shut off the exit to the ramp, keeping the way clear of other passengers, until a voice from the loudspeakers rasped out. First in German, and then in English. It said that the 1400 KLM flight to Amsterdam was ready to load at Gate 1. Passengers were requested to have their tickets ready.

Mr. Farrel was first in the line and first up the steps into the airplane.

3

AT FIVE MINUTES past two the next afternoon the high, stubby German bus slid to a halt in the gravel. The driver pulled the door open and pointed along a road that ran down a short hill to some low, flat buildings.

Packard paused at the opening. Over the roof of the large building he could see the steel frame of a diving board. A mesh fence surrounded the whole rear of the property. A river flowed beyond it. Beyond that the wet green hills.

"Airport?" Packard said. "Flughaven?"

"*Ja, ja,*" said the driver.

He made a circle over his head to describe a helicopter. Packard was the only one waiting to get off. The three other

13

passengers watched him frankly. They had the badly dressed up, overheated look of local villagers going to town.

He took one more look around at the sparsely populated outskirts of Bonn where they had stopped. A few red-tiled houses. A short street of small shops ahead of them. A dirt street. The lack of cars or movement.

He wedged his way out the door and started down the hill. The bus made a grinding U turn and headed back to the main highway leading out of Bonn to Cologne.

Three German boys in short leather trousers and open shirts stopped across the road and looked at him.

"Flughaven?" Packard called, still doubting.

"*Ja,*" said the largest of the boys.

They stood still and watched him as he moved on.

The buildings, when he reached them, were deserted. The wire gates were locked. So were the doors to the front of the buildings which the fence did not shut off.

Packard put down his suitcases and walked to the rear. Through the fence he saw a long, empty swimming pool. Beside it a patch of grass for games or sunbathing. There was no runway and no activity. On the top of the main building was the only indication that the place was of interest to airmen. A wind sock snapped fitfully under the flat gray autumn clouds.

Packard went around to the front of the building and sat down on his suitcases to wait. The three boys had come down the hill to where the road joined the parking area. They stood silently and watched him.

At twenty minutes past two, Packard said a dirty word out loud. He looked carefully around again in all directions. His hopes in the flapping wind sock faded.

At twenty-five minutes past two when Packard had stood up and lifted his bags, a Chevrolet station wagon with two men inside, and the blue and white crest of Sabena Airlines on the front doors, rocked around the corner at the foot of the hill and skidded past Packard with its brakes locked.

The driver got out and came back. He studied a sheet of paper on which Packard could see two names.

"You're Mr. Gray?" His American was colloquial.

"That's right."

"Glad it didn't rain on you. Come inside and let's do the papers. No one else is here?"

Packard pointed at the three staring children.

"Only those."

The other man had unlocked one of the doors in the front of the building and the steel wire gate. He had two small boxes in one arm and dragged a gray mail sack behind him

14

out of the door and through the open gate to the edge of the sunbathing field.

The man with Packard went into the bare room and sat down behind the bare desk.

"I thought I was in the wrong place," Packard said.

"No. You were right, but the service is new and small. May I have your passport?"

Packard took the green book from his breast pocket.

"Where does the helicopter land?"

"On the grass. It is more than enough. And if the engine fails there is the river for emergency. They try to build all heliports beside rivers."

"That's comforting. Am I the only passenger?"

"There is one other."

The men looked up and out the windows.

"But perhaps she will not come," he said. "It is all still irregular. But it is quite safe, you understand," he added quickly.

He stamped the passport and handed it back. He tore Packard's ticket. He came around the desk and lifted Packard's two bags. The wind rattled the windows and the sound was loud in the hollow room. The man made out baggage tags and tied them to the suitcase handles. Then he picked up the luggage and went toward the door.

"We will go outside and wait," he said. "The machine is due now."

It was twenty-five minutes before three.

Packard and the two Sabena men stood by the edge of the lawn with the suitcases and the cargo and waited. The wind was stronger and there was a scatter of rain with it. They all looked across the river and into the lowering sky.

"Perhaps it will not fly today," one of the men said.

"They said downtown it would fly," said the one who had taken Packard's ticket.

"Yes, but now the weather is worse."

"Helicopters cannot fly in clouds," the ticket man said to Packard. "They move in so many directions the instruments will not work. But I think the clouds are not yet too low."

They stood for a time in silence. Then they looked up quickly, all together. The helicopter was swinging in a wide, flat arc to stay away from the city area. It swayed slightly from side to side as it slowed down over the river for its approach. Sound came from its blades in chopping waves against the ground. When it hung directly over the field the grass lay matted and bushes around the lawn bent flat under the pressure of the rotors.

The pilot was in a hurry, worried by the weather. He did not touch the wheels of the helicopter to the ground, but held it blasting and rocking six inches in the air.

The ticket man ran to a spot below the high cockpit. He lifted a paper up on a long stick. The pilot read it. He pointed around and made a questioning gesture with his head. The man on the ground shrugged his shoulders. Over the noise no words were possible.

The cargo man shoved and pulled until he slid open the door in the belly of the machine. He helped Packard crawl up and over the sill, and secured the two boxes and the mail sack behind the front seats. Then the cargo man jumped down and waved at him. The ticket taker came to the door and saluted him. Together they pulled the door shut.

Packard slid the two halves of his seat belt across his lap. The beat of the motor grew to a pounding, howling roar. The helicopter shuddered and swung sideways. Then it leapt suddenly straight into the air.

Then, as suddenly, the power decreased. The machine shook in a convulsion as its direction reversed and Packard looked to see if they had made the river. The outside door abruptly slid open.

The cargo handler put a dark blue suitcase trimmed in white on the floor and a portable typewriter and a briefcase. The girl and the ticket man were hurrying across the grass. He was tearing her ticket and writing her baggage tag as he walked. She looked intently at the helicopter.

Her brown hair was cut in short Italian style. Her face was thin, but her mouth was not small and her eyes and eyebrows were nearly black. She was wearing a loosely belted British trench coat over a dark blue tweed skirt and a white Oxford cloth shirt. Packard had seen her picture with long hair. This was better. She was a very good-looking girl.

At the door the Sabena man handed her her ticket and baggage tag. She started to pull herself into the helicopter with the two men on the ground helping. Packard leaned over and lifted her into the cabin.

He shouted over the engine, "Welcome aboard."

She pulled her trench coat straight and glanced at him without smiling. She looked around the swaying cabin uncertainly and made an effort to hide her concern with the weaving floor and jarring noise by a too casual look of not noticing it. Finally she moved quickly and sat down in the seat next to Packard's window seat. Packard sat beside her and they wriggled into their seat belts. The ground crew slid the door shut. The increasing roar of the engine filled the cabin. The machine leapt again into the air and swung out across the river.

16

On the forward wall, a telephone connected with the pilot above. There was no other contact between cockpit and cabin. But even in this privacy there was no reasonable chance for Packard to talk over the bellowing noise of the machine.

He sat looking down at the ground a thousand feet below. The German countryside rolled green and gentle. Open fields were interrupted by the red-tiled cluster of a village; then fields; then a village, one narrow street usually, with the flat walls of brown stucco houses coming out to the edge of the roadway.

Chickens and ducks penned behind the houses scattered in hysterical white explosions across the yards as the helicopter passed over. The old and new fear of an enemy from the sky seized each group of tame fowl that they flew over.

The broad gray surface of the Rhine River carried traffic in swift streams. Cars moved fast on the shining wet double parkway of the autobahn between Bonn and Cologne. A few had their headlights on.

When he saw the twin red spires of the cathedral of Cologne from his window ten minutes later, Packard turned his head toward the girl.

"Take this," he shouted.

She could not hear his words. She glanced at him indifferently and looked past him.

He tapped on his window, indicating the cathedral. She turned her head and looked out.

"Take this!" he shouted again, close to her ear. He pointed at his seat.

She shook her head without looking at him, but she leaned half in front of him, as far as the seat belt would let her move, to look out at the Cologne spires.

Packard stared at the back of her head with his lips pressed together. The Cologne heliport below them was a new flat building. There were two squares of white concrete in front of it for landings and take-offs, connected by a narrow runway. Above the river the pilot changed the pitch of his blades so that the machine shook softly and began to settle uneasily toward the ground. The girl looked around quickly, then sat straight in her seat with her hands folded in her lap. The white faces of the people around the landing field stood out from their dark winter clothes. A gas truck waited to one side. The helicopter settled with the thick soft feel of a jump into a vat of ripe fruit. The pilot cut the motor. The quiet, with only the slow chop of the stopping blades, was heavily painful.

The girl began to slide the end of her seat belt through the lock.

17

"How long do we stay here?" she said, watching her small hands on the belt.

"Fifteen minutes."

"I can do without that buzz saw for fifteen minutes."

She stood up and pulled her trench coat straight and ran the fingers of her left hand through her short hair. She stood in front of the door.

"How do we get out of this diving bell?"

Packard was on his feet, leaning forward so that his head would clear the cabin ceiling.

"Don't worry," he said. "Someone will open it. They have to get the mail out."

She looked over her shoulder and studied him bluntly with her eyes. Then she turned back to the door and stood with her feet apart, waiting. She began to arrange her soft hair with the fingers of her right hand.

Packard twisted his mouth and shook his head.

The cabin door rolled open. A Sabena attendant in dark blue uniform looked at his passenger list and then up at them. He saluted.

"Good afternoon. This is Cologne."

"We saw the church," the girl said, trying to get through the door.

The attendant looked up at her. He finished his prepared speech before moving.

"There is a stop of about fifteen minutes. Passengers are asked to get out while the machine is fueled."

He tucked the clipboard under his arm and put the steps into place and offered his hand to the girl to help her out of the plane.

"You may smoke beyond the white line," he said.

A crewman in white overalls unrolled a gas hose from a truck and stuck its nozzle into the tank opening in the side of the helicopter. He ran a ground wire to protect against electric spark. Another German lifted the mailbag from behind the seats and dropped it carelessly onto the ground.

Packard walked a step behind the girl to the white line. She opened her flat blue purse and took a cigarette from a red package and lit it and looked around the field with rapid interest.

"And where are you going?" she said suddenly to Packard, finished with her survey.

"Brussels first."

"What are you doing over here? Making Europe safe for Democracy?"

"I'm not in the Occupation, if you mean that. I'm a student."

18

The loose brown waves of her hair came to his shoulders. She looked up at him.

"A student? Of what? Aren't you pretty old to be a student?"

"Everyone says so today. I'm a high school teacher. On leave to study over here."

He smiled. "Aren't you pretty young to be a famous reporter? I read the Carter papers."

"Well, good for you."

She held her cigarette between her thumb and first two fingers, pointing straight out from her hand. She drew on it shortly and blew the smoke toward the ground.

"If you read them well, you'll know I don't work there any more. They gave me a leave of absence. That's American free enterprise for canned."

She ground the cigarette out on the asphalt and put her hands in the pockets of her trench coat. Packard kept his smile.

"Don't get sore at me," he said. "I'm just part of the reading public. Are you going to Brussels?"

"Just for tonight. Tomorrow Amsterdam.

"So am I."

"That's nice," she said flatly.

She watched the activity around the plane. A Sabena representative had climbed up to the cockpit of the helicopter and was talking to the pilot. An elderly lady was being helped toward the plane by a man who looked like her son. The gas attendant still leaned against the hose. The crowd of spectators around the field swelled steadily.

Finally she said, "Is that where you are going to be a student?"

"No. I have two weeks before I start. I'm just traveling. Are you going to work over here now?"

"I haven't been run out of the country yet, if you mean that," she said to him. "As a matter of fact I'm having trouble getting away from it. I'm waiting for permits from our State Department, and they're taking their own sweet time. They're stalling."

She said aggressively, watching Packard's face, "I want to go to Moscow."

"I envy you," Packard said, without surprise. "I'd like to see Moscow myself."

She waited for him to say more. Packard looked at her small face, tense and ready to be angry. He grinned.

"It isn't a pleasure trip," she said. "I want to write a book."

The gasman was through with his job. He rolled the hose

19

back onto the truck. Packard watched the old lady in black dress, black hat, black shoes and black stockings as the man who looked like a son and the Sabena representative helped her into the cabin.

The wind was cold against Packard's face. He stepped to the side so that his back was to it and so that he was between it and the girl. She looked surprised and her face relaxed and she moved around to face him.

"What kind of book?" he asked.

"About the Russians. About what they are. Instead of the stuff we think they ought to be. Which is all you can write in America at the moment."

The Sabena attendant motioned toward them. They walked slowly back to the door and Packard helped her into the helicopter. The Sabena man was arranging the baggage behind the front row of three chairs. The little old lady was belted securely and determinedly into Packard's window seat. The man who looked like her son had the overcared-for smooth round red appearance of new business success. He stood in the middle of the cabin and watched Packard with careful defiance while he said goodbye to the mother.

Packard guided Sarah into the opposite window seat. He uncrossed the seat belt folded over the middle seat between Sarah and the old lady and sat down. The German lowered himself heavily to the ground, still looking at Packard, waiting for him to try to reclaim his seat. The mother turned and stared out of the window beside her. The Sabena man saluted and slid the door of the cabin shut.

Packard pulled the seat belt tight and felt that the girl was looking at him and he turned his head and said to her seriously, "I'd like to hear about your book, Miss Borsen. History is my field. Modern history. I'll take you to dinner in Brussels tonight if you'll tell me about it. Unless someone is meeting you."

"No one meets me these days," she said matter-of-factly. She looked aggressive again. "Are you married?"

"No indeed."

"Indeed?" For the first time she nearly smiled. "All right. Why not? Thanks."

The Pratt and Whitney engine began its starting whine. Packard looked through the window beside the girl and saw that the wind had torn a hole in the solid gray of the clouds to the north. For a moment there was a bright blue patch, but then it closed in again tight.

The aircraft began to shudder, the screaming blades making it weightless, ready for flight. The girl turned her face from the window and said something.

"What?" Packard said loudly.

20

She shouted, "What is your name?"

Packard saw her glance toward the old lady and he saw that she was stubbornly resisting the embarrassment she felt.

"Packard!" he shouted, and laughed at her expression. "Packard Gray!"

4

THE WIND between Cologne and Maastricht was steady from the northwest against them. In Maastricht an excited priest boarding the flight for Brussels found his baggage overweight. They waited and he repacked to cut out weight and save the money. It was twenty minutes past five when Packard stood in front of the desk at the Cosmopolite in Brussels. Half an hour late.

"Good afternoon, Mr. Gray," the clerk said. "There is a reservation. May I have your passport?" He looked at it and took an envelope from a pigeonhole behind the counter. He handed it to Packard.

"This came this morning for you."

He motioned to a bellboy and handed him a key. He pointed to Packard's bags and gave the room number in French—119.

"Your room will look onto the square," he said to Packard. "It is a single with bath. Is that not right?"

Packard said, "I wonder if you have without bath?"

"Of course," the clerk said. "But in your wire . . ."

"I know. But I have been thinking of the cost."

He was a student. A student would think of the cost.

"Of course."

He exchanged the key and the bellboy walked toward the elevator.

The room was large. Thick red draperies and a pink flowered wallpaper gave it a rose glow in the gray light of late afternoon and made it feel cheap and warm and protective from the weather outside all at the same time. There was a double bed, a wardrobe that stood out from the wall, a bureau, a desk below the windows facing on the square and, in the corner, a porcelain washbasin. On the desk was an advertisement for Brussels and the Hotel Cosmopolite. There was a blue overstuffed chair and a straight-backed chair with a blue padded seat.

"Where are the moving picture houses?" Packard asked the bellboy who was putting the suitcases on a stand.

The boy pointed out the window to the left.

"Straight along that street, sir. The Boulevard Adolphe

Max. And the Boulevard Anspach. The Place de Brouckère. Those are some of them."

"How long does it take to walk to the Royal Palace?"

"Twenty minutes. Perhaps half an hour."

Now Packard thought he could ask it without calling attention to it. "And to walk to the Grand' Place?"

"Only ten or fifteen minutes."

It was thirty minutes past five.

"Is it very beautiful?"

"Very beautiful, sir. Even in Paris there is nothing like it."

"Have you been to Paris?"

"Oh, often," the young man said.

"You are fortunate."

"I like to travel. I have also been to Germany and even to Holland, too."

"How do I walk to the Grand' Place?"

"Just as to the cinemas. To the left out the door, along Adolphe Max and Boulevard Anspach to the Bourse. A large gray building with columns. Left on this side of it and you will come soon to a church on your left and then the Place. Anyone can tell you. And it is lighted at night. There is no way to miss it."

"Thank you," Packard said.

The bellboy stood by the door. Packard took two German marks from his pocket. About fifty cents.

"Will this be all right?"

"Certainly, sir. Thank you."

When the door closed, Packard locked it. He walked around the room and looked at the one floor lamp and at the desk lamp. He climbed on a chair and looked at the ceiling fixture. He looked behind the single picture and around each piece of furniture. He stood and looked down at the telephone. There was no way to tell about a telephone until you talked over it and heard the buzz. And then maybe not. Especially when there was a switchboard. There was that possibility but no other sign of wires or bugs. In the walls, perhaps, probably not. He took the telegram from his pocket and read it. BUT OF COURSE NO OBJECTIONS HAVE A GOOD HOLIDAY WITHOUT END MOMS.

The message was right. The signature authenticated it; that and the word "but" within six words of the beginning of the message. He crumpled the envelope and put it in the bottom of the wastebasket. Then he opened one of his suitcases flat on the bed and one on the stand. From one he took the book. From the other he took a red necktie.

It was twenty-eight minutes to six. Packard washed quickly, and shaved. He tied his necktie and ran a wet comb through the brush of his hair. Then he put his shaving kit on the glass ledge above the basin. He put a writing pad on top of the desk, and he took a short steel ruler from the breast pocket of his sports coat and carefully measured the distance of several articles in the two suitcases from each other and from the edge of the bag. He measured the distance of the writing pad from two edges of the blotter. He did the same for the shaving kit. And he measured the position of the envelope in the bottom of the wastebasket. He noted the distances on the back of the title page of his book.

After that he shook a small mound of talcum powder onto the palm of his hand and blew it gently across the top of the desk and the notebook. He shook it again and blew the powder in a fine layer across the exposed contents of the suitcase on the stand. The maid would undoubtedly move the other one anyway when she turned his bed down for the night. He tore the body of the telegram into small bits and left the room.

The corridor was still empty as he turned toward the elevator. When he passed the public toilet, he stepped in and flushed the pieces of the telegram away.

The sky was nearly dark when Packard stepped into the noise of the street, and the wind was cold and blew in gusts. Automobile lights were on. Rows of cars were parked to his right in the Place Rogier and to his left the intersection of the Boulevard du Jardin Botanique and the Boulevard Adolphe Max was a jam of bicycles and people hurrying in the dark. A policeman in white gloves and a white rain cape moved his arms in patterned gestures. The traffic started. Stopped. Hurried. Slowed. Packard turned left from the hotel and waited for the right gesture. He crossed the intersection to the broad neon lane of the Adolphe Max. On the other side he stopped and waited for the people who had crossed with him to move on and disperse. No one paused or delayed. He studied the street sign as his excuse for standing. When he was alone, he walked on.

He moved along in the early evening excitement of the boulevard. There were strong emotions for him to this hour in any major city. Mostly sexual. Anticipation and emptiness, hope and a prospect of loneliness. He remembered with sudden anticipation that he would be with Sarah Borsen later, and not alone. It was something to look forward to at this hour, even under the circumstances. The lights of restaurants and shops were bright. Passing conversations were hurried and charged. Even the reflection of the street lights against low clouds was intense. Inviting and threatening.

Just before Packard came to the bright triangle of the

23

Place de Brouckère he looked into the fashionable, carpeted lobby of the Hotel Atlanta on his left. Sarah was staying there.

Brussels in this part had a modern feel at night. The Place de Brouckère with the needle of the Anspach monument in its middle looked like Times Square. Flashing signs, width, traffic, noise.

Packard walked past the flat governmental hulk of the post office. He stopped across from the Bourse, the stock exchange building, and looked up at its columns toward the cupola. Just as casually he looked across · the Boulevard Anspach, then back the way he had come. He saw no figure detached from the pattern of the street, no one too casual, no one looking pointedly away.

Packard looked up for the street sign and turned left on the Avenue de la Bourse. He jogged right when he came to the church and entered the Grand' Place through the narrow channel of the Rue au Beurre.

A few cars were scattered across the cobblestones in the center of the square. The high elaborate tower of the City Hall rose on his right, its gold surfaces glinting in the night lights. Along the left, the white lights of expensive shop windows and restaurants glistened on the sidewalk.

Packard walked a short distance into the center of the ancient market place and looked slowly around. There were only a few people. The bar for his meeting, the Roi d'Espagne, was just to the right of where he had entered the square. Its fireplace filled the enterior of the room and the street outside it with a red, wavering glow.

Packard let his eyes swing past the leaded windows of the bar and the recessed door without stopping. He turned to look up past the dozens of arched windows and the balconies and spires of the City Hall to the clock high in the tower. He looked at his wrist watch. It was two minutes before six and the rain had begun. No one had followed him into the square yet. He walked slowly toward the door of the Roi d'Espagne. At one minute before six he went through the door.

A few couples sat along the wall or at tables to the rear. A pretty, dark waitress came up to Packard and led him to a bench against the wall on the left of the entrance and pulled the table out so that he could slide in. He put his book face up in front of him.

"A glass of red wine, please," he said.

"Yes, monsieur," she said. "You are American?"

"Yes."

"That is a good thing."

"Thank you."

24

She went to the rear of the room. Past the stuffed dead horse beside the stairway that led to a balcony above. Packard looked up. Through the smoke that escaped from the glass sides of the fireplace the puppet figures of brightly dressed pirates swung by their necks from ropes.

The waitress brought the wine and a smile.

"That is a handsome horse," he said.

He pointed to the shaggy worn animal on its wheeled platform. The English was too much for the girl. Packard repeated in French. She laughed.

"Is that the horse of the King of Spain?"

"I do not know," she said, "but it has been here a very long time."

"Well, that's a clue."

"Do you like your wine?"

Packard tasted it. It was dry and full. It had the deep color of a young beet. And it was warming and right for the coldness outside.

"Very much," Packard said. "Is this an open wine? An ordinary wine?"

"Not exactly. I borrowed it from a bottle."

"You are very kind. Is there no danger?"

"I enjoy it to borrow it that way."

A customer called further down along the wall and the girl turned away. Packard looked at his watch—four minutes past six. And at four minutes past six the door opened. A swell of smoke went up from the fireplace. A menu took off from a nearby table, climbed a few inches, then stalled out and fluttered to the floor. The man who came in wore a gray tweed overcoat and no hat. His hair was black and thick and Irish. He had a pipe held in his teeth and he looked around the room as he pulled off his overcoat. He walked directly to Packard's table and held out a big hand.

"Packard," he said. This is fine. Pleasant trip?"

"Fine," Packard said.

They shook hands.

"It's been a long time, John."

"Oh, very long indeed."

He squeezed in beside Packard as the waitress came back to move the table.

"A martini vermouth," he said.

The waitress went toward the back. Packard looked at the big man beside him.

"I think your pipe has gone out," he said.

The man took the pipe out of his mouth and looked in the bowl.

"So it has," he said. "Do you have a match?"

"I think so."

Packard laid a book of paper matches on the table. The man picked them up. Packard began slowly to gather himself as he opened the paper cover. He thought of the man's size and of his own. They were close enough.

"Hell," John said. "I burn my hands on these things. I'll use one of my own if you don't mind."

He took a kitchen match from a coat pocket, struck it on the bottom of the scrubbed white planks of the table top and sucked the flame down onto the tobacco. The waitress put the vermouth down and hurried to another table.

"That better?" he said.

Packard's mind and body began to relax.

"You have a marginal sense of humor," Packard said.

"It keeps me going. You Washington types all take your tradecraft so seriously."

"It keeps us going," Packard said. They both smiled.

"By the way, you didn't leave your passport at the hotel, did you?" John asked.

"No. The clerk gave it back when I came out."

"You sure you got the right one back? I·have a friend who lost one that way and he missed a whole vacation waiting for another."

"I'm pretty sure."

Packard reached in and took out the passport. He opened it to his name, then the picture. John glanced over his shoulder.

"It's mine," Packard said. "I thought so. There aren't many Americans traveling this time of year."

He put the passport away. John took a sip of his vermouth. Packard let a swallow of wine sit on his tongue and felt the weight of it, drying.

"You remember Nicolas?" John asked. "Have you seen him lately? I was with him in Belgrade just after the war, you know."

"I heard it," Packard said. "I saw him only a few days ago. He's in good shape."

John leaned back against the wall.

"Now that we're formally introduced," he said, "how's your tour getting on?"

"That depends."

"Have you made any friends?"

"I met Sarah Borsen in Bonn. In Cologne I asked her to dinner tonight and she said yes. In Maastricht we set the hour. I call for her at the Atlanta at seven-thirty."

"How is she?"

"Very good-looking. Small, but it's all there."

John sipped his vermouth, then put his pipe back between his teeth.

"That makes it nice. What else? Did you like her? That doesn't matter so much. Did she like you?"

"We aren't engaged. She's a big-shot reporter who keeps acting as if she's afraid the editor will find out she's a woman, and I'm a poor student who might be better than nothing for dinner. And she's sore at the good old U.S. of A. It was a short flight, you know. And noisy."

Packard finished the wine in his glass. John was watching him past the bowl of his pipe.

"Why?" Packard asked.

"Because she's your assignment."

"What do I do with her?"

"That's up to you."

Both men smiled.

"Well, now," Packard said, "I guess someone has to do the dangerous jobs. The tough and dirty ones."

The waitress came past the table.

"More wine?" she asked.

Packard said, "Out of the same bottle?"

John shook his head.

She smiled. "I'll see if I am able," she said, and went off.

"What's that?" John asked.

"A local joke. She steals from the rich and gives to the poor. Now tell me about Miss Borsen and why she rates this kind of attention."

John followed the waitress with his eyes, waiting for her to bring the wine and leave them without interruption.

"What I wonder," he said, "is how you rate giving it to her."

"Proper attitude, devotion to duty, flawless behavior. Things like that," Packard told him.

John scratched a kitchen match and held it to his pipe.

"Ah," he said. "I see. I understand how they overlooked me."

The waitress put the wine in front of Packard.

"It's the same," she said. "But that is all I can get."

"Many thanks. I'll make it last."

She waited, but Packard turned his face to John and the girl went away to stand in the center of the room.

5

JOHN LEANED his head on the wall behind the bench and turned his face only slightly toward Packard.

"Washington wants you to stop Sarah Borsen from going back into Russia," he said with his voice soft but natural.

"Going back?"

"She was in there on an assignment about a year ago. Now she says she wants to go back and write a book on the place."

"She told me. That's how I got my date. We're going to discuss the book. Why doesn't Washington stop her if they don't like it? All they have to do is hold her permits to apply for Russian visas."

"Well, they don't stop her because State doesn't want the hand of the American government to show in this at all. The Department has stalled on giving her a permit to apply for visas as long as they feel they can. They're under steady pressure from all sorts of honest and otherwise civil liberties groups to quit restraining Borsen's Constitutional rights and let her go. The cable of instructions from Nick for you says they will probably give her the permits soon."

"Why shouldn't they? Is she a Communist?"

"I don't know. The FBI might know. If they do they haven't told us. So probably not. But if she isn't she's doing a job for them anyway. Everything they do is right according to her. If we do the same thing it's all wrong. She says so, too, in columns syndicated all over the country. Did you read her?"

"Not much. But I know what you mean."

Packard watched his hands around the stem of the glass.

"Still," he said, "there's a difference. If she's an enemy and you can prove it, you ought to lock her up. Or shoot her. If she isn't, or you can't, don't hound her until you make her one. I thought Nick felt that way too."

"I don't think we have to worry about how Nick feels," John said.

Packard looked at him. The statement had sounded pompous.

"I worry about everybody these days. A lot of staffs and papers and military and diplomatic people who are in a hurry can get between Nick and what he knows. Okay. What's the story?"

John took his pipe out of his mouth long enough to take a drink, then put it back.

"Well, Borsen was the syndicated property of Old Nate Carter and his newspapers. Until he fired her. After she came home from covering Korea a couple of years ago she got farther and farther to the Left with her stuff. It kept getting worse. He couldn't talk her out of it so he fired her."

"She says it was a leave of absence."

John twisted around toward Packard with his elbow on the back of the wooden bench.

"So?" he said. "Well, either way, she didn't quit easy.

28

She left with a lot of noise and martyrdom and there were plenty of people to loan her a soapbox."

Packard watched the red ghost from his glass wiggle on the smooth white planks of the table. He lifted the glass and let the heavy wine dry against his tongue before he swallowed it. John went on.

"She made the big circuit. Lectures and interviews and articles. She called the firing McCarthy police censorship. She said she claimed that she couldn't make a living in America any more. It made news for quite a while."

"I was away."

"Well, wherever you were it was probably being printed around you. The Red press made the most of it all over the world. Anyway she topped it off by announcing that she was going back to Russia to write a book, and she took off and moved into Switzerland to wait for the visas and permits.

"Then State heard from the FBI. They had gotten a tip that as soon as Borsen is allowed to enter Russia, she will ask for political asylum."

John reached across with his right hand and poked a finger into the bowl of his pipe, tamping the tobacco down. He drew on the pipe experimentally and got smoke, and leaned back.

"You see it?" he asked. "If they give her the travel permits and she asks the Russians for asylum, it will make them look good and it will make us look very, very bad. Especially in Asia and the Far East where this kind of trouble is big news. If they don't give her the permits they get a lot of public criticism for being restrictive and punitive. That's bad too."

"Did State check with her to see whether the tip is true or not?"

"They're afraid to approach her. If she hasn't thought of aslyum, they might give her the idea. If she has, she's apt to claim that State is persecuting her and interfering officially with her personal business. Anyway, they've made their decision.

"They are going to give her the permits. But they called Nick and asked him to lay on a special operation to intercept her. Unofficial. Showing no trace of American government interest. That's the main thing. Berne cabled that she had expressed trunks and luggage north from Switzerland and moved out of there, so she can be on her way in. It's your job to stop her."

Packard said seriously, "In any way I can?"

"No violence. No force. It isn't that big. No official capacity. Anything else."

29

"What else is there? Reason?"

John squared himself around on the bench. He looked sideways at Packard and smiled.

"Only one thing comes to mind immediately," he said. Packard did not smile

"I thought of it," he said sourly.

"Even if she doesn't go back in," he said, thinking, "can't she sit out here and ask for political asylum?"

"She can. But she'll be just another griper. Out here she can always change her mind, too. And out here the press from all over the world can still talk to her and come to their own conclusions. Once inside she can't change her mind, and only the select will interview her and give out whatever suits them."

"Did State ask Carter to take her back?"

"I don't know. The cable didn't say."

"You might wire Washington and suggest it. Once in a while they overlook things like that."

"Okay. I'll have Lois send you an answer in Amsterdam if you've left here. Don't count on it though. Everyone called Carter a Red before he fired her. Everyone calls him him a Fascist since he did it. He's had enough if he's smart."

"Probably. But let's do it the easy way if we can. A Carter job offer would be a lot more concrete than my boyish charms."

"Unless she's too sore to go back to Carter."

Packard finished the red wine in his glass and pushed the glass away from him, across the planks of the table, almost over the edge. He sat up straight with sudden impatience.

"I don't like the assignment," he said. "I'm a country boy. A bridge blower. Political action. I said it before. If she's guilty of something, grab her. If she isn't, leave her alone. When this outfit starts going after citizens who disagree with what the politicos want them to say, we're following bad examples."

John did not take up the discussion.

"You're here," he said, "at the right time, with good, new cover. All you're expected to do is talk her out of it."

"I'm here to look for die-hard Krauts who want to set up the Fourth Reich. I like that better."

"You'd better get used to this," John said, unimpressed. "It's going to be a long cold war. The spook business will spend more of its time from now on making our side look good and their side look bad than it will sabotaging shirt factories or brewing up revolutions. It's the new look. We're trying to outsell the competition. Not outblast it."

"I heard about it when we gave up Korea," Packard said,

feeling the beginning of anger in him. He changed the subject. "Are there any details on this Borsen assignment? Where do I make contact?"

John put a match to the bowl of his pipe. His face slowly relaxed. He looked around the room incuriously, then dropped the smoking match into a metal ash tray and leaned his elbows on the table.

"You are to look out for a man named Farrel," he said evenly. "Roger N. Farrel. I have a description of him for you."

"I already have it. He's fat and unpleasant. He was on my flight from the States. I saw him elbow his way onto a plane for Amsterdam yesterday. What about him?"

"He owns some newspapers and a publishing house called the Future World Press. Washington says that he is regarded as dangerous and you will avoid all contact with him if possible."

"What is he dangerous about?"

"It wasn't spelled out. He is going to publish Borsen's book on Russia. You are also to try to determine the connection between them."

Packard and John smiled at the same time, looking at each other, the antagonism relaxed.

"I will avoid all contact and make a full report on his relationship. Right?"

"I told you the instructions came from Washington. They made them up in the summer heat."

Packard looked at his watch. It was six-forty.

"I have a date," he said. "Is that all of it?"

"Almost all. Nick is putting someone into Amsterdam to help you if it comes to that. Someone outside the regular staff there."

"Who is it?"

"I wasn't told. The cable says that whoever it is will contact you if there is a need. The contact name will be the same as for communications—Lois."

"Who decides on the need?"

"Since the contact is one way, from Lois to you, I guess Lois does."

"This is Nick's way of keeping me a good boy, I guess. I sent the last helper they gave me away in a sampan and they lost him. When you cable Washington ask Nick to spare me the shadow.

"You might also tell him," he added, "that I don't like the work and I may cable him when I make up my mind about the girl."

John looked surprised.

"You really want that sent."

"Just that way."

John shook his head.

"Okay," he said. "It's your neck."

"It's my neck. It's everybody's neck if we're going to play that way. Who's next?"

John tapped his dead pipe on a metal ash tray. The small clatter silenced the few other people in the room momentarily. He drained the last slow heavy drops of yellow vermouth from his glass.

"When you get to Amsterdam call Ralph Dickson at our embassy in the Hague. He's a Third Secretary there and not one of us. He's a State Department boy but will probably know enough not to start talking over the telephone. You will keep in touch with him. He'll know who to call if you need something from us, and State wants to be kept informed on this whole operation since it is being run for them. You will probably want to get your own room in Amsterdam so that you can be close to the target."

"That a quaint way of putting it."

Packard began to hunt in the pocket of his trousers for money. With the other hand he motioned to the waitress.

"Let me get it," John said. "This is a business expense. It goes on the taxpayer."

"Yeah, but I get per diem. Well, go ahead. I still don't have any Belgian money."

"Want some?"

"No. I'll pick it up at the hotel."

The waitress scooped a handful of coins and bills from her pocket and counted out the change on the table.

"Leave her something more than the service," Packard told John in English. "She gave me extra attention."

John put a bill in the girl's hand. She smiled at Packard.

"I hope you will come back," she said.

"I think she's ready to give even more," John said.

"Thank you," Packard said to the girl. "You have been very kind. I will be back when I can."

The girl walked back toward the fireplace, looking over her shoulder. Packard slid out from behind the bench. John stood up and began to get into his overcoat.

"Where shall I take Sarah Borsen tonight?"

John laid his pipe on the table.

"Try Les Six Jeunes Hommes," he said. "On the Rue des Six Jeunes Hommes. Number 14, I think it is. It's expensive, but I like it, and it has a very conducive atmosphere. With music. Noisy enough to be private. Quiet enough to talk in. Look out for that street, though. It's blind and you can get trapped in it."

"Who's going to trap me? Sarah?"

32

"I don't know. I thought I'd mention it. I'll call your hotel tomorrow to make sure you've gone. If you stay around Brussels, you can call 19-26-29 each evening between nine and nine-thirty if you need me."

They stopped in front of the door. John held out his hand.

"Good hunting," he said.

They shook hands.

"Thanks," Packard said. "Don't forget to send my cable to Nick."

"I'll take care of it."

Packard opened the door. Smoke rolled over the glass shields of the fireplace. The waitress coughed. Two men sitting in a corner where the draught caught them looked around annoyed.

"You left your pipe on the table," Packard said.

John smiled.

"I know. You go on out and walk back the way you came. I'll give you a minute or two, then follow along to see if anyone has taken an interest in you yet."

Packard nodded.

"Good," he said. He looked closely at John. "Very good. I hope we run into each other again somewhere. Thanks again."

He stepped out onto the sidewalk pulling the door shut. The November rain was heavier and colder. The lights reflecting off the smooth oily cobblestones of the great square were blurred and stretched. He took a breath of the sharp wet air to clean the old sweet smell of tobacco smoke and stale beer spilled on wood out of his body. He counted six people hurrying along the wet streets going from light to shadow to light as they moved past bright windows. He glanced once, finally, to the right at the towering shining golden mass of the City Hall tower. Then he walked left to the Street of Butter and turned left again into the sudden blackness of the narrow alley.

6

PACKARD WALKED into the lobby of the Atlanta at seven-forty. There were drops of muddy water inside the entrance on the soft green carpet. A brown wood counter on his right, piled with stacks of pamphlets, where tours were arranged and tickets sold, formed a narrow entrance corridor with the wall on the left. The porter behind it nodded at him briefly. Beyond, on the left, the curtained doors to the dining room stood open. A subduing atmosphere of white cloth, silver, and formally dressed waiters escaped from it and made the lobby less public.

He stopped beyond where the corridor widened into the full lobby and looked around. Sarah Borsen put a magazine back on a pile in the rack before her and came toward him with short quick steps. She was carrying her trench coat and wearing a small rain hat. Both dry.

"Hello," Packard said. "Sorry I'm late. Were you going on without me?"

"Not yet. But I've been waiting."

"That's good. It shows a proper attitude," Packard told her.

She glanced at his face and looked down and began to unfold her coat.

"It's nice you approve," she said.

Packard held her trench coat while she put it on.

"I like your perfume," he said. "Come on."

He took her arm and started toward the entrance. He steered her aside to let two men shaking the rain from their hats go by. One of them, a flat-faced man and big, turned right and stopped in front of the desk. The other walked slowly to the magazine rack and stood with his feet apart looking at the covers. He stood there with one hand in the pocket of his thin tan raincoat. Dark patches of the cloth stuck to his heavy rounded shoulders where the rain had soaked through. His hair was straight and blond and too long. His face was full and childish and rosy-cheeked.

Sarah pulled her arm free.

"Wait a minute," she said.

She walked away from Packard, fishing in her blue handbag. She put the key on the desk between the clerk and the man he was talking to. The clerk smiled.

"Good evening, Miss Borsen."

Sarah came back to Packard.

"All right, I'm ready."

"So," Packard said. He looked past her as he spoke, at the two men. "Well, I've done preliminary research. I have a place in mind."

He turned her by the arm and they walked toward the entrance.

"That's good," she said. "I haven't been here before. I hope it isn't too fancy." She looked up at him defiantly. "I'm traveling on a budget. And I'm not working."

"I know. You told me," he said. "I asked you for dinner."

"I have an old habit. I pay my own way. It makes it better for everyone."

"You mean it makes it easier for you."

34

Packard grinned down at her as they walked along the entrance corridor.

"Then you don't owe your date anything at the end of an evening. Relax and enjoy it. I won't put in a bill."

"For the dinner or the analysis?"

A youngster in the uniform of the hotel ran out from behind the tour desk ahead of them and swung the door open.

"Taxi?" he asked as they reached the door.

"Please."

The boy trotted ahead across the sloppy sidewalk; through the heavy early crowd of the wet evening; out onto the street. He began to whistle and wave one arm up and down. Packard stood with Sarah close behind the door outside, under the canopy, waiting; until suddenly he felt the pressure of the opening door against his back. He moved aside with Sarah to make a passageway. The rosy-cheeked young man from the magazine stand shoved through the door and stopped abruptly on the sidewalk beside them and looked around. Packard and Sarah moved out to the curb, and the man walked a step behind them. The bellboy, with his hair dripping, motioned them toward the open door of a stopped cab.

"Taxi!" the rosy-cheeked man shouted. He still had one hand in his pocket.

Packard eased Sarah to one side with the pressure of his body. The bellboy held up his hand and whistled shrilly. A second cab slammed on its brakes in the traffic and began to back recklessly.

"Please," the bellboy said to Packard. "You will take this cab."

"The lady wishes to walk. Give it to this gentleman."

"I what?" Sarah said. "Take the cab!"

Packard ignored her. The bellboy shook his head. The driver leaned across the right hand seat and looked out the window to see what was happening. The second driver began to honk his horn.

"No. No. This cab is yours," the young man beside them said in French. "You have asked for it."

He made a move to take Packard's arm.

"We don't want it."

"But you called first."

"We don't want it."

The man hesitated on the curb.

"Please, sir," the dripping boy called.

The driver moved back behind the wheel and put the cab in gear. A crowd of people had begun to stop and watch and block the sidewalk. The driver of the second cab was

35

honking steadily now. The rosy-cheeked man glared at Packard and Sarah. He stepped off the curb and snatched the door out of the hand of the boy and slammed it shut behind him as he got into the seat. The cab ground away to the north on the Boulevard Adolphe Max.

"Oh, well," Packard said. He smiled at Sarah. "Let's take the other cab. All these people seem to expect it."

"Let's do something anyway," she said, "and not stand out here like crazy American tourists."

He led her to the taxi.

"Don't be embarrassed," he told her. "They won't remember us in the morning."

He helped her into the cab, and turned to the boy who was still watching confused. He stuck a bill in the breast pocket of his uniform coat and pushed against his shoulder.

"Get out of the rain," Packard said to the boy.

He paused on the running board of the cab while the boy who was drilled in duty above discomfort held the door for him.

"Now," he said to the driver in French. "Stop blowing your horn and take us to the Menneken-Pis."

He got into the car. The driver snarled. Without a look he wheeled the cab around in a slipping swing through the startled traffic, hunched over like a Cossack whipping his horse, he raced back toward the south.

Packard struggled for balance and settled himself in the seat. He looked out the rear window in doing it. No car had turned to follow them.

But the man with the childish face had certainly come out of the hotel after them. And certainly he wanted them in the first cab so that he could follow in a second. Too bad. Well, it had started. And where was the friend of Rosy Cheeks? The flat-faced one who had come into the hotel with him and stopped at the desk?

"Does he have to go so dammed fast?" Sarah asked angrily. "You made him mad when you yelled at him."

"You're still embarrassed. He was angry before he ever saw me. It's an occupational hazard with taxi drivers."

He leaned forward on the worn leather as the cab slid around the monument in the Place Brouckère.

"A little slower please. We want to see your city," he said. "Will you go through the Grand' Place?"

The cab driver gave up a fraction of his speed but stayed hunched over the wheel without answering.

"Well, it didn't help to yell at him."

"Did I yell? I didn't mean to."

"You might think how these people feel," she said. "The little ones like this who work all day in a storm. With people like us sitting back here ordering them around. Do you suppose they like it?"

Her voice was solemn and intense and reproving.

"I'll think about that," Packard said, keeping his tone pleasant. "Why don't you think about it's night, in a town you've never seen, and you're going out for dinner. Look out the window. This is the Grand' Place, the main square. Look at it. It's beautiful."

In the dim light she looked at him, surprised and wondering. Then the driver slowed to cross the great square, and she turned her head reluctantly and saw what was outside the window and twisted her body rapidly and moved her dark head to look at it. She bent nearly double to see through the glass on Packard's side at the tower of the City Hall.

Packard glanced quickly through the rear window. Theirs was the only vehicle moving on the surface of the square. He leaned forward and spoke to the driver. The taxi swerved to the curb and jerked to a halt in front of the City Hall.

"Come on," Packard said. "Let's get out and look at it."

He helped her out and paid the driver. They stood together and watched the taxi slide across the stones of the square between scattered cars. It turned left on the opposite side in front of the dark mass of the Maison du Roi and sped back in the direction it had come.

"Is this the end of the line?" she asked.

"No. But this is fine to see. I thought you would want to get out. The rain won't hurt. We're waterproof. Anyway he was a gloomy figure. We can get another one."

Could and had better. It was time to change cabs. Let them trace the other one here if they could. Let them spend their time searching this place. Packard looked at his watch. Seven-fifty. They had an outside ten minutes before anyone waiting at the Atlanta could ask the driver where he had dropped his fares. If the driver went back to the Atlanta. Or if the bellboy had heard his directions and repeated them.

Packard followed her into the middle of the square. Two policemen lounged against a car fifteen yards away, barely visible, and watched them momentarily. One of the police pointed at them and indicated the night and rain, then they bent away to talk together in the rain. Their white capes and white gloves glowed faintly in the center darkness of the square.

To the left firelight flickered from the Roi d'Espagne. Across the square from them, along the north side, the shop lights burned. Packard could see through leaded windows to the copper and paneled wood and shine of glass of a bar on the corner. At the opposite side from the Roi d'Espagne a small group of people crowded down the entrance steps under the bright lights of a cellar shop that was selling fried potatoes and fried meats across its counter. Behind them the flood of light burned brassily in the rain against the golden face of the City Hall.

Sarah turned slowly and looked from one side to another. Finally she said absently, "How did you know about it?"

"I walked here this afternoon. I talked to the people in the hotel. They told me I ought to see it. I like to find out about a city. And I wanted to have something special to show you tonight."

She had been looking at the lighted shop windows across the square. At his statement she turned back quickly and looked up at him; while the rain fell past the brim of her small hat and ran down her upturned face, past her dark eyes and red mouth.

"Did you really think of that?" She asked it seriously, as though he had to answer her under oath. She had her attention fixed on him so strongly that Packard was uncomfortable.

"Are you always so thoughtful?" she asked again.

He reached out and took her arm and turned her toward the center of the square.

"Don't make it so big," he said. "I guess I'm not. You told me I was bad with the taxi driver."

He started her moving with pressure on her arm and walked beside her.

"I was rude."

She walked a few steps looking down at the cobblestones. Then she raised her head.

"Take me over there." She pointed across the square to the bar on the corner. "Let's have a drink."

Packard looked at his watch. His ten minutes were more than up. It was eight-two. He glanced around quickly. The pattern had not changed. But he was anxious with a sense of time. He saw a taxi, beyond the policemen, its parking lights on, the driver sprawled behind the wheel.

"The place we're headed for is only a short ride. Let's go there," he said. "Do you mind? There's a cab."

"I don't mind."

As they walked up to the car, the cabdriver moved over to the right. He reached back and swung the door open for them. Packard put the girl in, then sat back, pulling the door shut behind him. The driver waited with his face half turned to them, a cigarette hanging on his lips, for instructions.

Packard opened his mouth to speak. But before he got the first word out, a black Citroën sedan turned sharply into the square at the west end. It slowed abruptly, close to the curb, and stopped in front of the Roi d'Espagne. A man got out of the front seat of the car and pushed in through the bar door. The car moved off, turned in front of the City Hall and came toward them.

Packard watched the car, already sure from its actions, disgusted with himself. He had known his limits and exceeded them. Sarah sat back in her corner of the seat, looking out of the window which her breath was misting, waiting. The driver sat with his arm across the back of the seat, waiting.

Packard laughed. Sarah looked at him.

"You've nervoused me," he said to her. "I started to tell him where to take us and the name is gone. Forgotten. You did this to me."

For the first time she smiled at him. Even in the dim light Packard saw her dark eyes watching his face with pleasure and for the first time her expression was soft and not guarded. He looked past her, through the window.

The black sedan had stopped opposite them, thirty-five yards away, in front of the City Hall. A man got out of the back seat and walked quickly around the shadowed edges of the square toward the group of people crowded under the lights of the fried-food shop. The driver climbed out and started into the center of the square toward them, turning his head, stopping to look into the parked cars as he came. Packard could make out the light tan raincoat and the heavy rounded shoulders of the man from the hotel.

"Now let's see," Packard said.

He leaned toward the driver who had pushed his leather cap to the back of his head.

"A friend of mine told me of a restaurant near here. Now I do not remember the name of it," Packard said to him in French.

"That will make finding it harder, monsieur."

"Thank you. I had thought of that. But perhaps you can help me. The address was on a street with a name and a number.

"As is usual."

"I mean that the name of the street had a number in it."

"Ah." The driver took his arm down and turned away. He leaned forward and started the motor of the cab.

"What are you doing?" Packard said shortly. "Don't drive yet!"

The driver pulled the lever down on the meter. It began a steady ticking.

"While we are talking, monsieur, I am out of service the same as though I were driving."

"Ah," Packard said. "I understand. It is the same thing."

"Was it the Rue Joseph II?" The driver turned back.

"No. No, that was not it."

"The Embassy of Liberia is in the Rue Vilain the Fourteenth."

"No. That is not the street or the name of the restaurant."

"Thank you, monsieur. I will think again."

"We'll have it in a minute," Packard said to Sarah.

"It might be easier just to go to the bar on the corner there."

"Too easy."

Twenty yards away the tan raincoat raised from looking into the windows of an American sedan. Packard saw the childish face as it caught sight of the cab. The man started toward the taxi.

"Now," Packard told the driver. "Get ready to start when I tell you. I want to go to the restaurant Les Six Jeunes Hommes. Don't start yet and don't turn on your lights now. Do you understand?"

The driver frowned at Packard, puzzled and surprised. Then he shrugged his shoulders. He turned away and pulled the long gear lever into low.

"As you wish, monsieur." He patted the meter to show Packard he didn't care what went on so long as the meter ran.

Packard leaned far back into the cushions beside Sarah, out of the line of the window.

"How's your French?" he asked her.

"It isn't."

"Well, the name came back. I broke your spell. We're ready to go."

She looked out of the window beside her. The driver was looking in the same direction.

"What is he waiting for now?" she asked nervously.

"He's warming up the meter, I guess."

Ten yards away and headed for the cab, the raincoat slowed to stoop and look in the back seat of a parked Renault. Packard, starting to lean toward the driver as soon as the man stooped, saw the policeman come up behind the car before Rosy Cheeks did. The young man straightened up to find the police standing beside him and froze suddenly. He stood stiffly. He posed in front of them with injured dignity. Then he explained rapidly, with gestures. He shook his head hard. The white-caped policeman remained motionless. Rosy Cheeks pointed to the Citroën and to his friend coming back across the black cobblestones from the fried-food shop. He looked around, trapped.

"Now!" Packard said sharply to the driver. "Let's go. But so as not to startle Madame."

The driver turned his head from the side window. He switched on his lights and let the clutch in and swung the cab in a U turn to the right between two parked cars. They left the square immediately, twisting upward through the narrow brick streets.

Sarah had her elbow on the arm rest, holding her chin in her hand, with two fingers along her cheek.

"This is a bad night for me with taxis," Packard said gently. "You aren't sulking, are you?"

She turned her head.

"No. Why should I be? I'm thinking."

"One can be as much trouble as the other in a pretty girl."

He looked around the back compartment of the cab.

"Do you mind if I roll down the window on your side to clear the steam off the glass back here so that we can see something? The rain would come in on this side."

"I'll do it." She started to bend forward.

"Stay there."

Packard reached across her. His body rubbed lightly against hers as he cranked the stiff window down three inches.

"There."

Sarah did not move away from him. He turned his head and his face was very close to hers. There was no movement except the bouncing of the cab. The tires whined on the wet street.

"Well," Packard said slowly. He left his right hand on the window knob. "That's open enough. The air smells good. It smells like nighttime in Europe on crooked dark streets and two people."

"Yes, it smells that way."

"Not too cold?"

"Not too cold."

"Still thinking?"

"No. I don't think so."

"That doesn't make sense, you know? I like your voice. It's bigger than you are."

"That's good. It's the only one I have with me."

She sat looking at him with her dark eyes open wide and her lips apart as if she was suddenly surprised. Not defensive, not resisting. But surprised to hear what she was saying and surprised at the low, intense way the simple words she said came out.

The cab turned hard to the left. Packard was thrown away from her. He caught himself with his right hand against the right window and pushed himself back into the seat on his own side, looking at her as she looked at him.

"Well," he said again.

Sarah lowered her head and began to search in her bag.

"Do you want a cigarette, too?" she asked him without looking up.

"I would, but I don't smoke. I carry them for tips and trading."

She lighted the cigarette with a windproof lighter and blew the smoke straight ahead of her where it eddied and then was sucked out in wisps through the open window.

"Did you see what was going on back there?" She was making an effort to be casual about it.

"Where was that?"

"Back in the square."

"No. What was going on? I saw a car stop and a couple of people get out of it. That's all."

"One man came almost to the taxi. Then the police stopped him."

She looked for an ash tray and finally knocked the ashes off onto the floor.

"What was he doing?" Packard asked.

"Walking along, looking into the cars."

"Well, that's a good reason for the police to stop him. I wasn't paying attention, I guess."

He looked out of his window.

"I don't know where we are," he said, "but we're still going up and it's darker out here."

"It was the same man that wanted us to take the cab at the hotel."

Packard turned to look at her.

"Are you sure?"

She nodded.

"That's funny."

She slipped the cigarette through the window and it went back past them in a red line. She wound the window shut and huddled back in the corner of the seat.

"You don't suppose he was looking for us, do you?" she asked. "After the way he acted at the hotel. And then being in the square."

Her voice was low and worried and she let the concern show openly in it.

"Why should he be? All we did was give him the first cab."

"Why did we?" She raised her head and looked at him.

"Because he was shoving from behind. If someone is in that much of a hurry, I like to get rid of him. What are you worried about, Sarah?"

She looked away, out the window, and did not answer. Packard smiled.

"Have you got a guilty conscience?"

"I've got something," she said so softly that it was hard to hear her over the wet tires and the noise of the old, climbing engine. "Nerves probably. It's been a bad four months. I thought someone was following me last night too, so I stayed in the hotel room all the time."

She hesitated.

"It's funny that you don't think there's anything strange in seeing that man twice tonight."

Packard said, "Now wait a minute. Don't start being afraid of me. If it was the same man I think it is strange. If it was the same man. Who would follow you?"

"I don't know," she said. "Unless it's the Americans, I don't know."

She took her red pack of cigarettes out of her purse, then dropped it back in and closed the bag with an angry snap.

"If I knew, I wouldn't worry."

"That was no American in front of the hotel tonight."

"I know."

Packard leaned along the back of the seat and put his hand over hers.

"I don't believe we go around following our own people," he said. "But whoever it is, if it's anyone, stop worrying about it tonight. Let me take care of you tonight. It's part of the service. It's a part I'll like, too."

She turned her hand over so that her palm was against his.

"I thought I could take good care of myself," she told him. "I've been doing it for a long time. But all right, you do it tonight. You look as if you could do it."

Packard straightened up but he left his hand on hers.

"If I thought it was dangerous, I wouldn't volunteer," he said. "But it's like a roller coaster. I don't think you have anything to worry about, and I'll get to hold you when the big dip frightens you."

She smiled at him again and closed her fingers over the back of his hand.

"I'll scream for you, too, when it happens," she said. But the trouble was gone from her voice and Packard knew she was not thinking much about the man in the square any longer.

"That will be fine," he said. "You scream, and I'll hold you tight."

43

7

THE CAB slowed finally and turned right into a street thirty yards long, narrow and without exit. A high gray wall blocked its far end. Packard saw the name of the street on a pole below the hanging lamp—Rue des Six Jeunes Hommes. The driver pulled to the left and stopped before a glass-paneled door. The gray glow from the door and the street light made only pale patches in the close heavy blackness of the street. The rain had become mist.

"Monsieur," the driver said.

Packard opened the door and helped Sarah into the street. He read the meter and gave some money to the driver. The man began immediately to count the bills.

Before he had finished counting he said reluctantly, grudgingly, "It is too much."

"It is not all tip," Packard said in French. "Part of it is to help you think of the other restaurant at which you left us if anyone should ask."

The driver looked again at the money in his hand.

"I remember the place clearly," he said. "It is in Waterloo. Monsieur will have dinner here?"

"Yes."

"Then I will go now to my house and eat also, which I must do at any rate. I will then return here and wait. I will not hurry."

"That's very good. It is a quarter past eight now. How about ten o'clock?"

Packard closed the door and the cab backed away. He walked with his arm through Sarah's to the door and opened it and they climbed the narrow wooden stairs that curved to the first floor and the bar. Three or four white wooden tables stood on the floor. A dark polished bar ran along the far wall opposite the staircase. A dart board with three darts stuck into the target hung on the right wall. Beside it more stairs wound up and out of sight to the second floor. The sounds of music and dishes and voices came down them. After the street the light was bright and reassuring. A bartender in a white mess jacket behind the bar and a middle-aged man in a dark blue suit and silver-gray tie with the weak look of indulged aristocracy sitting on one of the red leather stools before the bar were alone in the room as Packard and Sarah climbed into it.

The aristocrat stood up as they stopped at the head of the stairs.

"Good evening," he said in English. "Please come in. It is a bad night."

"Good evening," Packard said. "Not all bad, but this is pleasanter. May we have a drink and then some dinner?"

"The dining room is upstairs." The aristocrat indicated it with an underhand sweep of his arm. "We will bring the drink to your table if you wish it."

Sarah was looking quickly around the room.

"Where to?" Packard asked her.

"If we have the drink here," she said, "I can beat you at darts. I got pretty expert in Korea."

"All right," Packard said, "we'll have a drink here. What do you want?"

She glanced at the empty tables.

"Oh, let's go upstairs."

"The lady has changed her mind. We'll go upstairs."

The aristocrat smiled and bowed.

"There is more life," he said. "What will you drink?"

"A dry martini," Sarah told him. "Very dry."

"Two of them, then, please."

The man bowed again. Then he spoke to the bartender in French over his shoulder.

"George will make them in the American fashion," he said to Packard. "We have learned how to do it. Almost with gin only."

He motioned them toward the steps.

The room upstairs was a narrow L with the short wing to the left of the steps. At that far end two men were playing "La Vie en Rose" on a violin and an accordion. Dim orange bulbs stood in curved iron brackets around the walls and there was the spill of their light and the brightness from the bar below around the head of the stairs. The rest of the light came from candles that made each table an island in the shadow. A waiter in dress clothes led them expertly through the room and seated them facing the stairway on a cushioned bench against a wall where the eaves sloped steeply down. He opened a menu in front of each of them and walked away.

The couples at the tables on each side studied them briefly, then turned their heads away. Sarah finished a quick survey of the room.

"I like it," she said.

She put her blue purse beside her on the dark leather of the bench and lighted her cigarette.

"I like the Packard Gray guided tour. It goes to nice places."

Packard saw that it embarrassed her to say it. She picked up the leather-bound menu.

"What do you charge?" she asked brightly.

Packard leaned on the table with his elbows, his arms folded.

"Thank you," he said to the bartender who was carefully lifting the clear full martinis onto the table.

"Well, the charge varies," he said to Sarah. "We have a little different policy. The older the customer the more we expect."

"At least it's an honest policy." She smiled at him. "I suppose I can afford tonight, anyway."

He raised the martini.

"For special customers, special rates," he said. "Here's to Amsterdam and more of you."

She nodded, but the smile faded. She took a part of the drink and put the glass down. Packard watched her looking at the menu again and saw that she was not reading it.

"Let me order something," he said to her.

He motioned to the waiter.

"It's part of the tour."

"All right. Thanks."

Packard ordered quickly from the menu. The waiter picked up the folders and handed him a wine list.

"I use this one from the right-hand side, where the prices are," he said to her. Then in French, "Will you recommend for me?"

The waiter bowed and studied the list. He looked up at Packard. He moved his finger down the list.

"He just classified us as to probable worth. And taste," Packard said.

Sarah was looking away, to the right. Two tables from them a man in a brown and white sports coat of bright check had his hand in the air, looking down the room toward the musicians. He snapped his fingers loudly. The waiter started to say something to Packard.

"Hey!" the man in the checked sport coat called. "Down here!"

The noise of dining stopped in the room and heads turned toward him. The waiter glanced in his direction and turned his head back immediately.

"Hey!" the man repeated. "Music!"

He had red hair, tight on his head like a skullcap and a wide uncertain grin with too much wine in it. His wife, a thin pale woman with a tired face, said something to him pleadingly.

The waiter handed the red leather book across, marking a wine with his thumb. Packard looked at it.

"No," he said. "I know more about white wine. Bring us number 47, the Spätlese."

The waiter bowed again and turned away. The noise in the room resumed its uneven, interrupted drone. The musicians walked along the row of tables, sideways because the aisle was narrow. Sarah took a drink.

"American tourists," she said with disgust. "Every one a diplomat."

"Did you ever see a drunk German?" Packard asked her patiently. "Or an Italian? Or an Englishman? Especially an Englishman?"

He finished his martini and lifted the empty glass slightly from the table so that a waiter standing at the head of the stairs could see it. He raised two fingers.

"How long were you in Korea?" he asked her.

"Almost a year."

"What was it like?"

"Oh," she said sarcastically, "it was fine. It was a dandy war. They killed lots of Koreans and Chinese. And Americans, too. Everybody had a good time. You should see one."

"I've seen one," Packard said to her shortly. "But you were there as a woman and a reporter. A fairly rare combination. I thought you might have seen more to it than just a shooting match. That's why I asked."

"That's a good name for it," she said angrily.

She twisted around on the seat to look at him. Packard leaned back and folded his arms across his chest and watched her. She had made this speech before. She carried it with her, ready to use. He had pulled the trigger.

"A shooting match was just what it was. Between a lot of countries that didn't belong there. For something none of them wanted. And none of them needed. And nobody got."

"The Koreans probably wanted it," Packard said softly. "They needed it. And they got it. Or part of it."

"They got a lot out of it all right."

"A poor thing maybe, but their own."

"It would have been worth a lot more to them if we had minded our own business. We stuck our noses in and pushed the Chinese in and the Koreans got what was left. Which wasn't much, I'll tell you."

"We pushed the Chinese in?"

"What do you think we'd do if the Mexican army advanced on the Rio Grande?"

"I guess we'd send someone down from Washington to talk to him."

"Oh, that's very smug and funny. Unless you're a dead Chinese."

"Or a dead American."

"Thanks," she said and turned back to the table. "I know about those too." It sounded dramatized to Packard.

47

"You know a lot of things," he told her.

"I know about dead Americans," she said. "I was engaged to a marine in Korea. He's a dead American. If we had minded our own business, he wouldn't be."

"Ah." Packard looked at the side of her face with new interest. She had a deeply bitter expression around her mouth, but there were no tears. "I'm sorry to hear that."

"Why should you be sorry?" Her voice was low and she did not look up.

Packard put his hand on her arm. She did not pull it away, but her muscles were tight.

"If a person fights well for something, and he risks everything, and still he loses, that's reason enough to be sorry for him. And you should be sorry for him, too. Instead of yourself. If you think that way for a while, you'll get a better answer to what killed him than that he wasn't minding his own business. Which he was."

He patted her arm and took his hand away.

"End of lecture," he said. "Here. Drink this down."

The bartender put the wet glasses in front of them. The violin and accordion had moved down the room and stood in front of the table of the man in the checked sports coat, playing "Mademoiselle de Paris." The redhead was swinging one arm in time to the music and grinning foolishly at the musicians.

Packard said to Sarah, "He's having a good time anyway."

Sarah turned her head as she drank and looked at him. Packard glanced at his watch. Eight-forty. He could call John at nine.

"I guess he is," she said.

The redhead saw her watching him and bowed loosely in her direction. Then he stopped swinging his arm and stared at her. Finally he leaned over and motioned, with his hand open, to his wife to put her head close to his across the table. She listened and turned and looked at Sarah and lowered her head.

"Do you know them?"

She shrugged her shoulders.

"If I do I don't remember them." She put her half empty glass on the table. "Where are you staying in Amsterdam?" she asked.

"I don't know. I don't have reservations yet. I don't expect a crowd in November. How about you?"

"The Hotel de l'Europe. I hear it's a luxury place. But I'm meeting my publisher there and it's on his expense account."

"Does he have room on there for two? It sounds just out of my league."

She glanced pointedly around the room and looked at him with her eyebrows raised.

"Don't let this fool you." He finished the drink. "I'm still only a high school teacher. Or go ahead and let it fool you." he said. "It's supposed to make an impression. Who is the publisher? An old friend?"

"A new one."

"That's good."

She smiled at him, amused and pleased. "His name is Roger Farrel."

"Oh? He was on my plane from the States."

"Was he? He's going to help me get to Russia, I hope."

"What kind of friends does he have to do that?" Packard asked doubtfully.

"I don't know. But I waited in Switzerland for weeks for our so-called Department of State to give me permits. Until he finally wired and told me to meet him in Amsterdam and he would fix it up there."

Packard shook his head. "I don't know," he said.

"He seemed to know what he's doing," she said, quickly defensive. "After Carter fired me, Roger offered to send me back into Russia and publish the book I'm going to write. He's the only one who had the guts to hire me."

"That proves he knows what he's doing, all right," Packard said, kidding her. "But be careful."

"What do you think I should be careful of?"

"Of you. If I want to worry about you, you can at least help."

She shook her head with her full lips pressed together and smiled in spite of herself, and looked up as their waiter wheeled a high cart with a white tablecloth in front of their table. He lifted a silver dome from a silver platter that was kept warm by two candles under it and began to carve a Chateaubriand into thin red strips with restrained flourishes. He balanced the strips of meat on the blade of his knife and lifted them onto dinner platters. Another waiter pulled a cork from the chilled green wine bottle quietly and slipped the folded corkscrew back into his trouser pocket. He put the empty martini glasses on the cart and poured a little of the wine into Packard's glass. He waited while Packard tasted it.

"That's good." Packard nodded.

The man filled the glasses and put the cork back in the bottle and put that in a silver bucket of ice. The two waiters went away together, wheeling the cart.

The couple at the table to their right had stood up. They waited until the cart passed, the woman twisting to get into her coat. When the waiters had gone by, they stepped into

49

the aisle. They looked down at the table of the redheaded American who was fumbling with loose bills in his hand while the musicians stood in front of him, talking to each other, pretending not to notice the money.

The American raised his head in time to see the couple looking at him. He half raised himself, cramped between the bench and the table and bowed and made the motion of tipping an imaginary hat to them. He held the pose after they had turned their backs on him and headed for the stairs. Then he looked toward Packard and Sarah. He dropped some bills on the table for the musicians and began to struggle out from behind the table. His wife said something and he nodded toward Sarah.

"I think your friend is coming over," Packard said to her.

Sarah glanced at the man's back as he worked his way out between the tables. She took a drink of the white wine.

"I hope not," she said, frowning. She put the glass down and picked up her fork.

Packard watched him come unsteadily along the aisle, rocking suddenly from one foot to the other so as not to stagger into the tables on each side. He stopped in front of them with his hands in his pockets and cocked his head to one side, looking at Sarah, his eyes squinted. Packard put his fork down and smiled.

"Good evening," he said.

The man in his brown and white checked sports coat swayed in short, tight circles as he stood there. He did not look at Packard.

Finally he said, "Aren't you Sarah Borsen?" The esses were fuzzy.

It was between a question and a challenge and Packard quit smiling and leaned back, with his hands on the table.

"Yes," she said.

"I thought so," the redhead said with crafty triumph.

Packard looked at her and saw the blank effortful expression on her face as she tried to place him. The man saw it too.

"Oh, you don't know me," he said. Each word was lower down the scale than the one before it. He had a short wide face and he was pushing his chin out and up and looking down at her squinting his eyes still more.

"You don't know me. But I know who you are."

Packard said, "Well, that makes you one up. Suppose you tell us who you are."

The man turned his head slowly and looked at Packard as though finally giving attention to an unwelcome and annoying child. He stood like that until he rolled and caught his balance and faced Sarah again.

"Is he one of your Red friends?" he asked her. He jerked his head toward Packard.

"I'm from Detroit," he told her. "I've read all about you in the papers. I read that Commie column of yours, too."

He leaned over belligerently. His voice was loud and it carried. People at the tables around them stopped talking and looked at them.

"You're drunk," Packard said to him with his voice low. "And you make a bad impression. Suppose you go on back and sit down."

"Suppose . . . suppose you mind your own business, Comrade." He took a step sideways and leaned over the table, rolling his body for equilibrium. "I want to have a word in private with this lady here. This little Commie lady. You just leave us alone."

Packard raised his hand and motioned for a waiter. He felt his anger, close to the edge.

"I think your wife wants you," he said. "Why don't you go see."

"Don't you mention my wife's name!"

The man pushed his face toward Packard's and rocked his head with each word. Sarah's face was white and rigid. She still held her fork in her stiff, trembling fingers and sat with her eyes fixed on the man's red face.

Packard said in French to two waiters who had come up, "We don't know this man. He's drunk. Will you get him back to his own table? And keep him there?"

One of the waiters said to the drunk, "Please, sir."

He put his hand lightly on the sleeve of the checked coat. The man swung his arm back violently, hitting the waiter in the chest with his wrist.

"You Commies always have to get somebody else to do your dirty work for you, don't you?" he said to Packard.

He staggered and started to pull his coat straight with great care and study. The waiters started toward him. He motioned them away.

"All right. I don't need any help. I just want a word in private with this little Commie lady here."

He liked the phrase. He smiled and winked at the waiters. He stepped up in front of Sarah again.

"I'm an American," he said. "A real American." He reached out and caught himself with a hand against the table. "I'm glad. I'm very glad. I am extremely glad, little Commie lady, to see they finally kicked you out. And we hope you stay out." He raised his hand to point his finger at Sarah. "And all real Americans hope . . ."

He swayed back and came upright. He started to say more, but he had forgotten what else it was the real Americans hoped and he stood there glaring at them. Then he swung around and walked in shallow curves back toward his table, shaking his head, with the waiters following him.

Packard took a breath and let it out slowly to relax the muscles around his stomach. Sarah was staring down at her plate. She noticed the fork still held in her hand and let it down softly onto the side of her plate as though she wanted no slight noise to attract more attention. She put her hands in her lap and looked down at them.

Packard did not speak to her. He took the wine bottle out of its ice bucket and filled her glass and his own. He put her glass in front of her on the edge of the table. She shook her head.

"It never happened over here before," she said.

She raised her head. "Do you want to take me home now?"

He looked at his watch. Nine-fifteen. It was time to call John.

"Do you want to go home now?"

"I thought you might have had enough of me after that. I'd understand it."

She looked toward the redhead.

"The bastards!" she said, talking to herself.

Packard began to slide out from behind the table. She looked at him quickly.

"You wait here a minute," he said, "while I find the men's room. Then we'll go look for some lights and music. How's your dancing?"

"Neglected."

"Good. So is mine. You'll be all right here?"

She shivered once. Then set her face.

"I'll be all right. I've had it from better men than that."

"Oh? Well, maybe it's something you've said," Packard told her seriously. He was standing in front of the table now, and he saw her ready to answer and did not wait for it. "You sit tight," he said. "I'll be right back."

He walked across the room to the steps without turning his head and asked a waiter for the telephone. The man nodded his head down toward the bar.

"Will you see that Madame is not bothered again?" Packard asked him.

The waiter touched his chest and winced. He looked toward the table where the redheaded man was talking with many gestures to his pale-faced wife who sat with her head turned away from him.

"I myself will see to it, monsieur," the waiter said.

Packard smiled. "Look out for his backhand."

"Pardon?"

"Never mind. Thanks."

In the room below, Packard found the telephone, against a wall. Two ears of plywood made an open shell on each side of it. Semi-private. The aristocrat was gone and the room was empty except for the bartender. It was twenty minutes past nine when Packard put a coin into the slot and dialed John's number. At the fifth ring, a woman's voice answered and he pushed the speaking button on the face of the telephone.

"May I speak with John, please?"

"Pardon, monsieur?"

Packard switched to French and asked again.

"I am sorry, monsieur. There is no one here who calls himself John. May I ask who calls?"

"That is not of importance if John does not live there. Is this 19-26-29?"

"That is right."

"Then it is the number John gave me tonight. I was to call him there."

"I am sorry, monsieur. Perhaps John is a friend of my son who is not here. If you can leave a number I will ask on his return and you can be called."

Packard read the number to her from the disk on the telephone.

"I'll be here for only three minutes," he said. "After that it is not possible."

"Very well, monsieur. But of course I do not expect my son in three minutes."

"All right. Thank you. It is important."

Packard hung up and for some seconds thumbed idly through the telephone book on the shelf in front of him. Then he walked over to the bar. The bartender looked up.

"You are not busy tonight," Packard said. The bartender leaned on his bar listening to American jazz on the radio.

"It is the rain and the season."

"Your martinis are very good."

"Thank you."

Packard pointed. "How does one play the dart game?"

The bartender switched off the radio. He looked toward the round board on the wall where pie-shaped spokes radiated out from the center bull's eye, each numbered. The numbers went up to twenty in random order.

"There is one game," the bartender said, "that one begins with 301 points. You throw and subtract each number. The one who first gets to zero wins."

"Is that all?"

"That is only how one wins. It is not so easy."

With his elbow on the bar the bartender pointed down at the floor. "You stand with your toes at that line."

"It does not seem far. About two meters?"

"Yes. It is far enough."

Packard sat looking at the board.

"We don't see such a game often in America," he said.

The three minutes had gone. The music still came down from the dining room. Packard leaned away from the bar. The bartender switched his radio on again and turned up its volume. Packard walked to the stairs and climbed slowly toward Sarah. He was on the fourth step when the telephone rang in the bar.

He swung back down the four steps with his left hand on the rail. The bartender stopped at the back of his bar with his hand holding the half gate open, watching him with surprise.

"It's for me," Packard said over his shoulder as he picked up the instrument.

"Hello."

"Packard?" The speaker was breathing hard.

"Yes."

"What did you drink earlier this evening?"

"Red wine. Stolen."

"Good enough. Sorry I made you wait, but I don't talk business over the home phone. I had to run to the corner. What's up?"

Packard looked incuriously across the left plywood ear. The radio was still going. The bartender was back at his newspaper.

"Do we have anyone on this job but me?" he asked John.

"No."

"Are you sure?"

"This is my area. They wouldn't put anyone in here without telling me. Why?"

"Then someone else is playing too. They came into her hotel as we were leaving. One tried to follow us but I got rid of him. Then they picked us up again in the square. Three of them, including the one from the hotel."

"Where are you now?"

"The Six Young Men."

"Did you lose them?"

"They tangled with the police."

"Did you get a good look at anyone?"

Packard described the rosy-cheeked tough.

"He's the one I saw the most of."

There was a pause while John thought.

"I don't know him," he said finally.

54

Packard said, "Wait a minute."

A couple came down the steps beside him and saw him and quit talking. They went across the room and started down the stairs to the outside.

"Okay," Packard said. "I've tried to think why anyone else would be after her. I can't; unless she's changed her mind about going in and they plan to take her in anyway."

"I don't think so," John said. "That's rough stuff for what they'd get out of it. I don't think she's changed her mind, either. I paid her a visit tonight, after she left. I borrowed a letter out of her room. It doesn't sound as if she changed her mind. You'd better come out here, I guess, where we can talk about it."

"What's in the letter?"

"She talks pretty rough about home. I'll show it to you." John gave him an address on the Avenue Louise.

"Take a cab to the Place Louise," he said. "Then walk. It's five blocks out. Be careful. I have to live here."

Packard looked up the curve of the steps. He saw a woman's legs. Then a pair of slacks. Then a brown and white checked sports coat.

"Hold on," he said into the telephone.

"Seventy-five francs!" The redhead's loud voice echoed in the bar. The bartender raised his head.

"That's . . . why that's more than thirty-five dollars!"

"You had an awful lot of wine, Sammy," his wife said.

"Wine! Wine? Why, the guys that run this joint must think they've got a gold-plated . . ."

He looked over the side of the bannister and saw Packard. They came off the steps onto the floor.

"Hey, Comrade!" the redhead said, stopping. "You guys live pretty good, eh, Comrade?"

"Please, Sammy," his wife said timidly.

"Wait'll they catch you spending Party funds in here, Comrade!"

"Please, Sammy!"

"Okay. Okay!"

Packard kept his eyes on the man's face, saying nothing. Finally the redhead lowered his eyes and started his wife towards the outside steps with a push. As they disappeared down the steps, he shouted, without looking back,

"So long, Comrade!"

"Okay," Packard said into the telephone. "Where were we?"

"What's going on?" John asked him.

"A drunk. A real ambassador for America. I'd like about three minutes on my own time."

"You haven't got it. Keep out of trouble."

"I know. Thanks. What time do you want me?"

"Anytime after ten-thirty. I'm leaving for a contact right now. I'll be home then."

"I don't know," Packard said doubtfully. "The girl is already frightened. She said someone followed her last night in Bonn. Then this stuff tonight. She's on edge, and suspicious. It won't take much to blow me. I don't know when I'll get there. I have to get back to her now."

He looked at his watch. He had been gone ten minutes.

"I'll make it when I can."

"Okay."

A sudden thought made Packard lean toward the mouthpiece as if getting closer to John.

"What time did you go into her room?" he asked.

"Seven twenty-five. When she went down to meet you."

"Seven twenty-five! Then you were . . ."

Packard heard the heels on the wooden steps. He saw her good legs, then the blue skirt, descending.

"Watch out for yourself," he said urgently to John. "So long."

He dropped the mouthpiece into its cradle and stepped back, away from the wall, before she saw him, and went toward the foot of the steps to meet her.

He had not said enough to John. Had not had time to remind him that they had all been in Sarah's hotel together. John and Rosy Cheeks and especially his flat-faced companion; to remind him that Rosy Cheeks had gone out of the hotel and was accounted for, but that Flat Face had stayed inside. He had not thought of Flat Face again until it was too late. That restless part of his mind was anxious with warning, but it was too late.

He reached his hand up the last two steps and took Sarah's arm.

"Where are you going?" he asked.

She stopped on the floor beside him and looked up.

"You were gone so long," she said.

She had her coat over her arm.

"I didn't want to wait up there. I've had it. I got tired of being looked at. A lot of those people seem to understand English."

"Okay," Packard said, and took the coats. He helped her into the trench coat, and put on his reversible.

"I'll take care of the bill," he said, "and we'll go somewhere."

"I've done it already. Let's go."

She started for the outside steps, without waiting, her small body rigid as she walked. Packard stared for a moment at her back, then caught up with her and took her arm and walked beside her, feeling her tenseness against him, down the narrow, curving steps.

8

As soon as Packard pushed the door open for her he saw the cab, twenty feet to the right, under the misty light in the alley, not so dark now because the wind was whipping the clouds apart.

The driver was behind his wheel, shadowy in the reflected dash light, his head down, his cap pulled low on his forehead, his arms crossed stubbornly over his chest. The windows of the car were rolled shut and he had locked his door. Packard bent his head and looked closely to make sure that it was the same man who had brought them.

The redheaded American stood beside the driver's window, peering in, slapping the cab roof hard with an open hand and shouting belligerently. His wife had walked away, to the right, and stood near to the end of the short street, looking away. The cabdriver was hunched down in his seat, studiously ignoring the pounding and the shouting. Sarah stopped on the threshold of the door and pulled back against Packard's arm.

"Wait until they've gone, Packard," she said. "Please."

Packard drew his arm free from hers. He looked down and put his hand against her cheek and said, "Stand right here, Sarah, and don't be frightened."

He walked away from her to the taxi and touched the redhead on the shoulder.

"I think you're trying to get into our cab, Sammy," he said.

The man jerked around and looked up.

"Go to hell, Comrade," he said, and began to pound again on the roof.

The driver saw Packard. He sat up straight and pushed his hat back and unfolded his arms and rolled the window down a cautious two inches. He put his mouth up close to the crack.

"I have tried to tell him, monsieur," he called to Packard in French.

Packard nodded. He put out a hand and took the checked sports coat and spun the redhead around.

"Listen to me," he said. His voice was low and hoarse. "You've made enough noise for one night. I arranged for

57

this cab two hours ago. Go inside and call yourself another one."

The redhead dropped into an unsteady crouch with his fists clenched and wide apart.

"Oh yeah? Well, I don't take any orders from any Commie bitch or her boy friend!" he said loudly. "Now shove off, or I'll bust you!"

Packard was taller than the man by six inches and bigger.

"You might try that. I wish you would. But it wouldn't be a good idea." He felt uncomfortable, that in the way of such things it could get to be a long and loud and silly argument.

"I'm not afraid of you!" the man announced.

It was going to be that way.

"It's good not to be afraid of people." Packard kept his eyes on the man's face as he talked. "It's bad to fool yourself about it."

"Open the door," Packard said to the driver.

The man wasn't sure. He looked at the redhead.

"It's all right," Packard told him.

The driver hesitated again. Then he reached back with his left hand and pushed down hard on the inside handle. Immediately the redhead's expression changed to a sly look and he made a sudden grab for the door and pulled it open and held it back against his body with both hands.

"Alice Anne!" he shouted. "Hey! Alice!"

The thin woman down the sidewalk did not move.

"Come on! I've got him!"

The woman stood still. Packard motioned to Sarah who came off the stone doorstep, slowly toward them. The redhead crouched, holding the door, and the knuckles of his two hands were pale white with the pressure.

He looked at Packard, and Sarah walking, and at his wife with helpless, tearful anger.

"God damn you, Alice!"

All at once he pushed the door from him savagely and began to run with stumbling steps toward his wife, awkwardly, his fists clenched again at his sides.

Packard swung the door open and helped Sarah into the back. He closed the door behind them, and the driver started his engine and began immediately to back out of the Street of the Six Young Men. Sarah stared out of Packard's window.

"What about her, Packard?" she said anxiously. "Will she be all right?"

Packard watched the thin, pale woman as they came beside her. She stood still and straight in the shadows of the street with her arms wrapped in front of her, pulling her coat tight against the cold wind. She was looking at her husband who was in front of her, leaning forward, his feet apart, shaking both fists in the air beside her and yelling. She did not flinch and she was not answering. Alone with him she did not look afraid or timid.

"She'll be all right," he said to Sarah. "She's only afraid of what he looks like to other people."

He leaned forward.

"Take us somewhere," he told the driver, "where we can dance and where we will enjoy being together, and where there are no other tourists. Can you do that?"

"It is what all other tourists want, too. No tourists."

"Okay," Packard said. "Do your best."

He pushed back. Sarah was in her corner of the cab, her face almost against the window. Packard saw her shoulder shaking very gently.

"Come on," he said softly. "Don't think about it. We'll start over again."

"A Commie bitch and her boy friend," she repeated.

"Oh, damn," she said, crying.

Packard reached out and took her shoulders and pulled her steadily back against him, then dropped his arms around her. He felt the surprised stiffness in her body, then felt it relax as the wary tenseness crumbled and she let herself go against him.

Finally she said, simply, "I'm glad you're here, Packard. I'm very glad you're with me."

"If I hadn't been, none of this would have happened, though."

She nodded her head, leaning away from him briefly to pull a Kleenex from her purse, then coming back to him.

"It happens anyway. But it helps to lean somewhere.

"Not just anywhere," she added quickly to make him sure of what she was trying to say.

Packard's conscience was not easy, but he said, "We all need someone we can count on. The worse it gets, the more we need them."

"Do you? You don't look as though you have much need."

Packard tightened his arms around her. He rubbed the side of his face against her hair gently.

"Easy now," he said uncomfortably; "no hero worship."

"I think I need that too," she answered seriously after a pause. "It's been so long since I've had so many things. I made myself forget a lot."

She straightened up in his arms and wiped her eyes with the tissue in quick movements. She did not move away from him, but she said briskly, defensively, as though disturbed by the way the talk had turned, as if she did not want him to know too much of her, "Well, where does the Packard Gray tour for little Commie ladies go now?"

"Be still," Packard told her. "I like you better the other way."

9

IT WAS TWELVE-THIRTY when Packard and Sarah got out of the taxi in front of her hotel. The drizzle had stopped but a cold wind blowing in sudden, hurting gusts out of the west rose and fell in the quiet streets. The lights in the Place de Brouckère were fewer and the movement in the city was dying out. The smell of rain was still in the air but from time to time the high wind pushed the swollen cumulus clouds back and a patch of stars was visible. The brightness of the hotel lobby had been dimmed to night lights.

"Will you wait?" Packard asked the driver.

"But certainly."

They walked through the lobby. Sarah had her arm through his, leaning against him. A sleepy elevator boy rocked the two front legs of his stool onto the floor of the elevator and walked across the lobby to get Sarah's key.

"Do I have any messages?" She called it to him as an afterthought, still holding drowsily to Packard.

The boy turned back and felt into the high box.

"Nothing, madame."

"Thank you."

"Did you expect something?" Packard asked.

She shrugged and looked down.

"I guess not. I knew a lot of newspaper people in different places, but I don't often hear from them now. I haven't called anyone. It's just a habit to ask."

At the elevator door she said, "Are you coming up?"

"I thought I would. Is that all right?"

"That's fine. But I could get up alone, too. You have the cab waiting."

"He should be used to it by now. He's waited all over Brussels."

"He took us to all those dance places. He was nice, wasn't he?"

"You wouldn't let him quit."

The elevator boy walked past them and handed the key to Sarah and put his hand on the control lever. He shook his head, trying to wake up.

"I didn't want him to quit," Sarah said. "You're the one who gave up."

They got into the lift.

"I'm getting into shape slowly," Packard said. "I hope to do a lot of this in the next week or two. I like it."

She looked up at him and smiled with pleasure.

"Did you? That's good. So did I."

The elevator boy leaned against one wall and yawned as he closed the door. He yawned again when he opened it for them.

"I'll be right back," Packard said to him, and followed Sarah down the hall to the left, shuffling slowly, letting her set the pace. She looked relaxed and sleepy and smiled to herself.

The corridor was quiet and dim and empty except for the shoes, neat beside the doors. Around a corner they came to a door where a pair of blunt-toed man's black oxfords, a pair of solid brown low-heeled practical woman's walking shoes, and three pairs of children's shoes were lined up in descending order.

"How do you suppose they all sleep in there?" Packard asked.

"I don't know, but I hope they do it quietly. I live here."

They stopped at the next door. She held up her key loosely by two fingers and dropped it into his open hand. He took it and turned the lock. He opened the door wide and reached for the light switch on the wall. He pushed the switch down and stepped back. The room looked empty.

"There you go," he said. "Get a good night's sleep. I'll see you in the morning."

She did not go into the room, but leaned with her back against the side of the door, letting her blue purse hang straight down at her side in her left hand.

"Will you get on the plane?" she asked.

"Sabena. Ten-five. I'll try for it."

They spoke in the low tones that a hotel corridor, late at night, imposes.

"Anyway, I'll come to Amsterdam tomorrow. And I'll look for you at the Hotel de l'Europe as soon as I get there."

"You'll find me there, but try for the ten-five. If you're sure you're ready to leave Brussels, that is."

He smiled.

"I'm sure I'm ready to go to Amsterdam. And so are you. Stop fishing. I'll see you tomorrow."

He leaned forward, with his hands on her arms and kissed her gently and slowly. She did not raise her arms, or cling to him, but she kissed him in the same way, slowly and naturally and with great tenderness and certainty. When he stepped back, she opened her eyes and the look of surprise was on her face again.

"Do you want to come in?" she asked, without self-consciousness. "I can offer you a drink."

"I'd better not."

"No. I guess not."

She pushed him away from the door.

"I'll see you in the morning, Packard."

"You'll be all right? Stay in the room if you're worried and don't open your door."

Automatically she looked over her shoulder, into the room, with a sudden nervous expression.

"I haven't thought about anything since dinner."

She looked back at him.

"About being followed or frightened or yelled at in bars."

"That's good. Go on to bed, then. I think you were seeing ghosts anyway. Good night, Sarah."

"Good night, Packard."

He had gone five yards down the hall when she called to him.

"Packard!"

He wheeled abruptly, the muscles along his stomach going tight. She had put her head back out of the door and was smiling a smile that faded as she saw the set of his face and body. He relaxed when he saw the smile.

"What is it?"

"Everything is all right," she said. "I just remembered that I never told you about the book."

"We'll have time for that now," he said. "Good night."

He heard her door close when he was almost at the elevator. The boy was sitting on the stool again, leaning back, his right arm hooked over the control handle, asleep. Packard turned back and went along the hall to Sarah's door. He stopped and listened while she opened the closet door. Finally, he heard the water in the bathroom. She was alone in her room, then. No one had waited for her. He ran the distance back to the elevator.

The cab climbed to the right away from the flat center of the city up the first low rise to the east. The streets were narrow, somber with shadow. Shops crowded in upon the roadway. A yellow light in one fell on racked guns behind a steel grill. In another a blue vase and deeper shadows beyond.

The taxi curved left into a fork of wider streets, where two Gothic towers of a cathedral stood black almost to the tumored bellies of the clouds moving past above them. Cut-glass windows without light behind them were blank and

62

concealing. The opaque hulk of the cathedral had an evil feel to it in the wind and lateness of the night.

"What is it?"

"The Church of St. Gudule."

They skidded right, around a corner into a wide main street. On their left a flat expressionless park stood empty. Beyond it an iron fence surrounded a high gray block of building, lighted with floodlights, with many windows. Two sentries walked precisely along the front of the fence.

"The King's Palace," the driver said.

They had climbed to the lip of the hill now. In front of the law courts the driver bore right past a monument and slowed down at the curb. He pointed to a low wall.

"From here," he said, "Monsieur is able to look down on the whole of the city."

Packard leaned to the right window and looked out. A few lights, flatness, blackness; the darker blackness of a steeple.

"Perhaps tomorrow," he said. "It is too dark."

The driver drove again to the left across the open square.

"Even in the day it is not a fine view," the driver admitted.

"You'll get in trouble with the Chamber of Commerce."

"Pardon, monsieur?"

"The King would not like to hear you say that."

"Hah! The King does not stand there looking over. And here is the Place Louise, monsieur."

The driver pulled to the curb. He looked around him at the deserted wetness of the Place. "Monsieur has an address?"

"No. This is fine. What do I owe you?"

"You owe me more for waiting than for riding."

He looked at the meter and shrugged. He thought. He suggested a price. Packard began to count out the money.

"You have been very good," he said. "Many thanks."

"I thank you many times. Monsieur was able to make an impression on the lady?"

"Only an impression."

"Ah, well, one has time. There was no difficulty after the Grand' Place?"

"None. Again thanks."

Packard opened the door and got out.

"Will I wait again?"

"No. How can I walk back to the Grand' Place?"

"It is a long walk."

"That does not matter."

The driver gave him directions.

"Thank you."

"Good night, monsieur."

The driver looked around again. He put the car in gear. When he made a turn and drove off, Packard walked across the width of the Boulevard Waterloo, under the still dripping trees of the parkway, across the width of the smaller avenue beyond it and stopped where the Avenue Louise started east.

10

HE LOOKED carefully around. At that moment he was alone in the street. He turned and walked quickly along the Avenue Louise watching the numbers, the disturbance in his mind growing insistent. Nobody had waited in Sarah's room, but that was the place to wait for her. Probably he should have stayed outside the Atlanta to see if they went in when he left. No one had followed him from the Atlanta, but that was the place to pick him up if they wanted him. Why weren't they waiting for Sarah, after working so hard to catch up with her earlier? Because they suddenly didn't want her or didn't need her? Possible, but not probable. Something to do with the letter John had stolen?

The wind caught him in mid-step and blew him sideways on the walk. He went up a short flight of stairs to see a street number. He looked back and studied the shadows. He went on again faster.

Why hadn't they followed him? Because they knew where he was going? Impossible. Because they didn't care about him? Unlikely. Anyone with Sarah was of interest if they were after her. Again: because they knew where he would go? Not possible. But his mind refused it.

"Oh, my God," he said aloud.

They weren't after him because they didn't want him and didn't need him. It was that easy. They knew where to find Sarah and they knew where John was, and the letter. The letter must be as important as John had thought it was. If they weren't after Sarah at the moment, they were probably after the letter. Maybe they wanted them in that order. He began to run, the wind making his lungs hollow when he reached for air, his steps loud clapping in the residential silence.

He turned his head to search for numbers. He sprinted across a side street. Three blocks. John had said five. Two more. He looked at his watch and forced himself to walk. One o'clock. John had been home since ten-thirty. He was so late now it made no difference. They had come or they wouldn't.

It was the flat-faced man who came into Sarah's hotel with Rosy Cheeks. The man Packard had forgotten to report until too late. That's how they would know where John lived. That's the boy who had followed him home.

"I forgot," he said bitterly. "I forgot to tell him."

He said it half aloud into the wind. With disgust and anger. Then, as he thought about it, with fear. He began to run again, and he was three quarters to the end of the fourth block when he saw the black Citroën beyond the middle of the long block ahead of him. There were a few cars parked along the curb, half of them Citroëns, but he was sure. Again his mind knew what his eyes could not prove. He stopped running and walked close to the right edge of the sidewalk where the shadows were deepest, getting his wind back.

He turned right at the next intersection and crossed the street twenty yards from the corner. He came back to the Avenue Louise and stopped. Two men were walking down the short flight of stairs from a house toward the Citroën. They waited on the sidewalk. One of them turned to the car and seemed to say something. Immediately Packard heard the motor turning over.

Three of them. He took a deep breath and let it out. Now. He had sprinted five yards when the two men saw him. One yanked open the back door of the car and scrambled in. Sixty yards. The other man yelled toward the house and then bolted into the car. Thirty yards. A figure appeared at the top of the steps, looked toward the car and then at Packard and hurtled down the stairs. Four of them! The car turned left, pointed into the street, waited. The man was at the sidewalk, across it. He reached for the open door and Packard dived to tackle. The man held on to the door. Packard caught him around the knees, twisted, tore his hands from the door. The car started away from the curb, willing to leave the man. Packard grabbed for the body; his hands slid on the heavy shoulders under the tan trench coat; he jabbed with his thumbs for the little eyes above the rosy cheeks.

The blow of metal against his cheekbone was a blast of light then numbness and nausea. He made himself fight to his feet, made himself run. The car was moving down the street gathering speed. The man had caught it, and he hung on through open windows to the post between front seat and back. He half ran, half rode, trying to climb through a window. The driver continued to accelerate.

Packard stopped. The car was out of his reach. There was no license plate. He stood in the center of the street, gasping, nearly sick, real pain beginning in his face, and he saw it when the man lost his grip. He lit on his right foot, tried to run with the momentum, but his left foot hooked behind his right and he smashed to the pavement on his head. The force carried him end over end. He drove into the trunk of a parked car and slid backwards to the street, and Packard ran again.

The brakes of the Citroën shrieked. The two men clambered out of the back seat and dragged the body between them into the car. The driver stepped on the accelerator in low gear and the car raced off and turned the corner to the left, the rear door swinging wide.

Packard stopped, until he could not hear the engine, then turned back toward the house pressing his hand to his cheek. An upstairs window opened behind him.

"What is it?" a woman yelled.

A man from a first floor window in the house next door shouted, "What did he say it was?"

The woman, "He didn't say. You there; in the street! what has happened?"

Packard walked without an answer. He saw John's number on the house gate and he climbed the five steps to the open door with the light burning beyond it and went in. He pushed the door closed behind him with his foot and stood carefully looking around. He heard the woman's voice and got his direction from it.

"Oh darling." It was in English. "Oh darling, oh darling, oh darling." In a chant.

Packard walked past a dark carpet crumpled on one side of the narrow hall, past a coat rack with coats and umbrellas open, scattered beside the stand below it, through double doors on his left.

Bookshelves that covered the right wall had been emptied. Books littered the floor across that end of the room. Chair cushions were thrown down, the drawers of the desk opposite the door had been dumped. The embers of a fire were dying in a fireplace grate beside the desk. The thick green draperies on the left were drawn across the street windows.

A heavy straight-backed oak armchair was on its side in the middle of the room, a man still held in it, his hands handcuffed to the arms. A tall woman with disheveled short brass-colored hair in a thin dressing gown, ripped in two long tears and hanging, squatted beside the chair, trying to pull it upright with its limp weight. Her back was to Packard and she was chanting, "Oh darling, oh darling."

She was not aware of him before he put his hand on her shoulder. Then she twisted away from him and stared, trying to control her breath to make a scream, shaking.

66

"Please," Packard said soothingly. "Don't be afraid of me. I am a friend."

He turned away from her and bent over the chair, lifted the head and saw the face, the ugly crushed dent with much blood at the base of the skull. He felt for a pulse mechanically but without belief. John was dead. He touched nothing else.

He stood up and the woman hadn't moved.

"I was to come here tonight," he said gently, "to see John. Is anyone else in the house?"

The woman shook her head once and stared at him. He reached out and took her elbow and half helped, half lifted her to her feet.

"Do you believe me? Do you know who I am? I was to come here tonight and ask for John."

"Yes. You called. He said you would come."

She spoke some of the words on outgoing breath. Some in whispers as she sucked air in, with the rhythm of growing sobs.

"Will you come with me? To another room," Packard said. "And try to talk to me. The police will come soon, I think, and I can't be here."

She looked down at the body and whimpered. Packard turned her away and with light pressure moved her toward the door. She slumped against him and clung to him crying openly and hard.

He held her, letting her cry, moving very slowly out of the room. In the hall he pushed each of the doors loosely shut with his elbow and guided her across the hall into a dining room.

A sideboard had been emptied; drawers of silver and linen, shelves of china spilled on the floor; the rug turned back; a heavy table overturned to expose its underside.

Packard pushed the woman softly from him and lowered her into a chair. He pulled another chair close with the toe of his shoe and sat down. He still held both of her hands.

"Now, please," he said. "I understand. But try to talk to me. I have very little time. Try to tell me about John."

She took her hands from his and made an effort to cover her exposed body with her gown. Packard could still see the red and white pressure splotches left on her by rough hands.

"He said you would come here," she said. "If he wasn't back I was to let you in. When there was a knock on the door he wasn't home. I thought it was you. I came downstairs and opened the door. They just walked in."

"What time was that?"

"I don't know. After ten. But he said you would ask for

67

John. They didn't even know his name and I knew something was wrong but they wouldn't leave and they waited for Frank and . . ."

"Frank was his name?"

"Frank was his real name. He just used John sometimes. I can say that now, can't I? It doesn't make any difference now, does it? And I was his wife too."

"Yes, you can say it."

"They made me stay in there and they asked me for a letter that Frank had brought home and I couldn't tell them and they tore up the whole room. And then Frank came home and all four of them jumped on him and hit him with a gun and handcuffed him in the chair. Then they asked him about the letters and he said he didn't know anything about them and they began to hit him some more but he didn't have the letters and then they tore up the whole house. Like this. And upstairs, too."

"All four of them were in here?"

"There were four at first. They told one to go look in Frank's car then stay outside and watch."

The woman looked around the room with disbelief. When her eyes came to the door Packard could see her look through and out to the doors across the hall and beyond them. She started up. Then slumped back into the chair dully.

"Did they find what they were looking for?"

"No. They all came back into the den. And one of the men said he knew Frank had the letter because he had seen him come out of a girl's room and he followed him here. And then he went back and looked in the room and the letter was gone so he knew Frank had it. And Frank said there weren't any letters when he got there. The man said he knew Frank was lying and he told a big blond man to see if he couldn't make Frank tell him. And then . . ."

She stopped talking and looked at Packard as though she saw him for the first time in the room.

"Oh, this is a terrible business," she said. "People do awful things and they say it's for their country. And I was so proud of Frank and I thought it was so exciting. But it isn't. They do awful things. Did Frank have to do things like this? Do you?

"You look as though you could," she added sadly.

"I don't know," Packard said. "I don't know whether he had to do anything like this or not. He never had to do it this way. Nobody does unless he likes to. Please tell me what happened."

"The blond man began to grab at me and poke at me and . . . and . . . play with me and I screamed and Frank fought and the other two held him in the chair and he didn't say anything but just fought. And finally one man asked him who was the man with the girl and Frank said he didn't know. He'd never seen anybody with the girl. And they kept on with me. And finally the same man said there was too much noise and they had been here too long and maybe Frank was telling the truth. But if he wasn't they would be back. And they let go of Frank and told the blond one to come on and they went out. But the blond one didn't let go . . . and he started to . . . and Frank tried to run at him with the chair dragging and the man pushed me away and took a gun out of his pocket and waited for Frank and hit him horribly on the head."

She stopped the automatic recitation and remembered.

"And the other one had already told him to go and even after that he hit him."

She sat numbly and then remembered that she had been talking and finished it.

"Then they called from outside and he ran out and then you came."

She leaned over double in the chair, finished, sobbing.

Packard looked at his watch. Twenty minutes past one. If the neighbors had called the police he was running out of time. He lifted Frank's wife up by the shoulders.

"Listen to me," he said again. "Do you know where the letters are?"

"Oh no! I would have told them."

Packard had an urge to smile at the simple honesty of the statement, and held it back.

"Did Frank know anyone was here before he came in the house?"

"I had the lights on downstairs. I was supposed to do that if anyone was here."

"Did Frank say anything at all after he was hit?"

"Oh no! He just fell over and he never moved."

"After you told him I had called earlier tonight and he went out did he come back in again?"

"He only called from the door to say you would come."

"All right," Packard said. "I'll go now."

He put his hand on her shoulder.

"Do you have an emergency number to call? Did Frank ever give you a special number for emergencies? From OSA?"

"Yes."

"Well, those are his people. And mine. You must call them right away. They will tell you what to say. Do you understand?"

"Yes."

"After that, call the American Embassy. Do you know the Ambassador?"

"Yes."

"Then call him as soon as you have called the emergency number. Then, if they haven't come already, call the police. Don't go back into that room. Can you phone from upstairs?"

"Yes."

"All right. Do these things then. And you must not tell anyone that I was here. The neighbors have seen me come in. So tell the police and the Ambassador exactly the truth, but tell them a stranger ran in off the street to help and saw what had happened and told you to call the police and left. Do not say that it was an American. When the people from the emergency number talk to you alone, you can tell them everything, but no one else. Have I confused you?"

"No."

"You have it all? Sure?"

"Yes."

"What is your last name?"

"Anderson."

"You are brave, Mrs. Anderson. And Frank was brave. I hope I won't waste that. I would like to stay and help. I can't. But maybe I can do something."

"You can't help now. Nobody can help now. He's already dead."

"Yes. People can help. In time. We can't undo, but we can help. And with luck we can keep from wasting courage. But I have to go now. Is there a back door?"

"Yes."

She stood up, leaned on the chair, then began to walk.

Packard said, "Wait a minute."

He walked to the door and listened. Outside the house, the neighborhood was quiet, and the street.

"I'll go out the front way. If the neighbors are still watching they can see me leave. Go make those calls right now. I don't know whether you want to hear it or not, but the blond man who hit Frank is already dead. Or I think he is."

"Did you do it?"

"No. I haven't been much good tonight. His own people did it. Good night."

She stood still in the room.

"Go upstairs to the telephone!" Packard gave the order sharply.

She began to move, turned right, up the stairs. Packard went out the door and down the steps and into a night wind that now, at that moment, smelled fresh and clean and felt good against the pain in his face.

70

11

HE WALKED away from the house, away from the direction he had come. Then he turned left into a sidestreet and walked rapidly, keeping the red glow of downtown lights against the clouds to his left.

He had no choices now. He could only go back into the city. He had no hope of returning to John's house that night. Or Frank's house. One man and probably half a dozen names had died that night. Had been killed.

He had no choices to make and for fifteen minutes as he walked he let his mind run loose with the emotions that surfaced to be cleared or faced or filed away.

There was his own guilt. John was dead because Packard had been careless. Had forgotten to tell about the man in the lobby of the Atlanta. But then John was also dead because he had overlooked details himself. John had forgotten for an hour, for five minutes that he could be followed in this friendly city. That was the price of success and the cost of failure in his work. There was no final relaxation, no forgiven forgetfulness.

Packard bore obliquely, moving through the streets in a wide arc to the left. The wind was from his left now and calm except at intersections, because the houses and the dark, padlocked shops broke its force.

Pity for a young woman tugging without strength at an overturned chair, crying to a dead man in a sobbing chant, reciting her story in an anesthetic numbness that would soon break into swallowing grief came next into his mind, but he could not feel it wholly. He knew what it would be like, but it was not his.

Anger that he had to hold in followed, and fantasies of physical vengeance in which he could pound and hurt with his bare hands. The constant hatred, freshly polished, of a system and animal men who served it willingly seized him while he thought on what had happened. It fired him as it had each time he came against the men and their methods and kept him from quitting. Kept him from wanting to quit.

"Because they like it, God damn it," he repeated. "Because the bastards like to do it that way. Even to each other."

He put his hands in the pockets of his overcoat to stop a child's urge that came on him to hit the fluted green metal of a lamppost with his fist. He looked around self-consciously, because he had spoken aloud in the silence, and because of what he had wanted to do. There was no one else out in the wind on the empty streets. He looked at his watch, thought back on how he had come. He turned left and headed for the heart of the city.

And there was still Sarah. He still had to coddle Sarah, to woo her and lead her lovingly home down a State Department red carpet. To hell with the bitch. To hell with such a job. Maybe the redhead was right. A Commie bitch.

He had forgotten. John had been careless. But Sarah was the one who had brought it to pass. By stupidity. By strong, clever words used selfishly, unreasoning, to blame a country because she had lost a lover. To sell it out in wholesale female revenge. And she might end by getting herself killed too. Too bad, Sarah. Sorry, Sarah. Even if she didn't know what she was doing.

He slowed up on the street, and stopped, alone in the darkness, wondering why he had used those words to himself, without thinking. "Even if she didn't know what she was doing." How did he know she didn't? He had no proof that she wasn't working deliberately against her own country. Only because she didn't use the standard talk or the pat phrases of the real, hard-core ones? Because she attracted him? Not much proof.

It was the old warning to foreign operatives. Don't fall in love with your agents. Don't come to like them so much, or feel so sorry for them, that you let them lie to you or sell you to the enemy or turn on you. After what had happened in the house behind him, it was a warning to remember. To hell with Sarah Borsen. To hell with her, foolish or clever.

He stopped his mind's rambling abruptly. He had a job. Sarah was bigger game than he had believed. If she was worth so much to the Communists, she was worth that much to him. The State Department might be right. There was always an outside chance. He could work on her all right. He could do what he had to do.

He had come to a wide thoroughfare, the rue du Trone. It ended there in the sharp point of a triangle with the Rue Luxembourg on the Avenue Marnix. He could look on across the Boulevard du Regent and see the grounds of the King's Palace. He crossed to the Boulevard and turned right, walking on the west side and watching for a taxi. The dark sky was open, filled with the weak flicker of stars, cleared by the wind.

12

PACKARD got out of the taxi two blocks west of his hotel and walked back. If John's wife had done what he told her, he was not involved. But he would not take the chance that a taxi driver could read a morning paper and call the police to say that he picked up a foreigner at two in the morning and delivered him to the Cosmopolite. He did not have time for official talks.

A clerk came from a small room behind the desk when Packard called. His face was pale and loose, tired from the effort of sleep in a chair, unclean with growing whiskers.

"Monsieur?"

"The key to room 119, please."

The clerk half turned to the boxes behind him. He turned back.

"But Madame has it already."

"Madame? I'm alone."

"So we believed also. But Madame has arrived at one o'clock and said that you expected her to wait in the room. That you had told her to do so. We gave her the key, therefore."

"Yes. That is right. I thought she would not arrive so late. Thank you. Good night."

Packard turned and saw that the elevator cage was empty. He started away toward the stairs.

"Pardon, monsieur."

"Yes?"

"Pardon. But of course Monsieur understands that if the room is to be a double the price must be adjusted."

"Sure. Of course. I will talk with Madame."

"And we must have the passport and she must register."

"Naturally. But it is late. And if the price is to be higher by so much—"

"As you say, it is late, and while we may leave the formalities it is important to understand about the price."

"I do that. Good night."

"I will take Monsieur in the elevator."

"Thank you."

The elevator cables rumbled deeply in the shaft and the open cage banged flatly against the rails as they went up. They did not speak, and the clank and whir of the elevator machinery was the only sound in the dim building above the lobby floor. They stopped at the third floor. The clerk pulled the folding gate open. He looked at Packard under the glare from the round white globe in the top of the cage.

"You have had an accident?"

"I slipped in the rain and fell against the door of a taxi."

"Do you require a doctor?"

"No. I'm all right. Thanks."

"There is one in the hotel. He is not expensive."

"No, but it is kind of you to think of me. Good night."

"Good night, monsieur."

Packard's door was locked. He knocked and waited and knocked again. He heard a sudden stir of bedding.

"Who is it?"

"Packard."

"All right. Wait a minute."

The bedding rustled again. The bed creaked. She opened the door an inch and held it.

"Wait a minute now," she said again. He heard her get into the bed, pull up the covers.

"All right."

The lights were on in the room, overhead, and the floor lamp and the table lamp. The draperies and the wallpaper with its roses were not so warm, and cheaper in the artificial light. Sarah had moved his suitcase from the bed. Or a maid had. It was open on top of his other suitcase on the stand. She had moved his toilet articles above the basin over to make room for her own. Her blue leather suitcase was open on the desk and her briefcase was on the floor beside it. He would never know whether they had been through his room or not.

"Hi," he said. There was more anger, and disgust and suspicion for him in finding her in the room than surprise.

He pulled out of his reversible raincoat and opened the doors of the wardrobe. He hung it inside. He took off his sports coat and spread it across a hanger and hung it on the round wooden rod.

"Like it better here?" he asked flatly.

"Where have you been? What happened to your face?"

"I slipped on a wet curb getting into a taxi. The back door was open and I fell against the top of it. The driver took me to a doctor. He put hot pads on it."

"He must have put a lot of them."

"He did. He charged by the pad."

"Let me see."

Packard turned around, his mood making him stiff and unwilling to talk, and leaned a little over the edge of the bed without touching it, his hands on his hips. Sarah sat up in the bed. She just touched his skin on each side of the wound with the fingertips of both hands. Her expression was serious and worried. Raising her arms pulled her breasts high and tightened the thin pale blue nylon cloth of her pajamas against them; Packard felt the sudden hotness of excitement in his stomach. It came in spite of his anger and aversion. It made him want her when he did not want her at all. He straightened up.

"Did I hurt you?"

"Not much."

He walked over to his suitcases; put the top one on the

74

floor. He took a pair of pajamas out of the lower one and dropped them on the arm of the blue chair and sat down in it.

"It looks awful."

"It doesn't feel good."

"It's after two o'clock, Packard."

"I know."

"I've been waiting here for you since one."

"I know. The clerk told me."

Packard had his shoes off. He leaned over the grip on the floor and took out two aluminum shoe trees and put them in his shoes. He pulled his short knitted socks off. She was still sitting up in the bed bracing herself with her arms, her forearms twisted outward.

"I waited up until a quarter of two. Then I thought you might be out all night and I came to bed."

"That runs up the cost of the room."

The look of uncertain, anxious concern disappeared from her face with the shock of his words. She was astounded, then hard again, the professional reporter, defensive, scornful.

"Well, thanks, Packard. First things first, I guess. With Americans, it's money. I'll get out. Let me know what I owe you."

Packard remembered John and took her reaction without sympathy. Then immediately he thought of the assignment. He made as much of an apology and an excuse as would come out of him, unwillingly.

"Sarah, I'm sorry. That was bad. Let me tell you about it. I didn't expect you to be here. I don't like it. When a man is after game he has a right to go out and hunt it. If it comes to him, it's too easy and the kill disgusts him. He doesn't get a chance to prove himself. Something is wrong with it if it's easy. That's Puritan blood. I must have it, because that's the way I feel."

He pulled the knot out of his cloth tie and folded it and put it in the suitcase on the stand. He stood up and started to take off his shirt, and saw her face. Her eyes were wide open. She had clamped her teeth shut behind her closed lips and it drew her neck tight and flat. She took a deep, slow breath in through her nostrils. A long breath, getting ready. Packard pulled his shirt over his head and began to fold it into the suitcase. He did not look at her, but he waited. He lifted the top of his pajamas from the arm of the blue chair and pulled it over his head. He heard her let out the long breath quickly. Then he looked at her.

"All right, Packard," she said. She said it slowly, with a tone of great common sense, logic and justice.

"All right, Packard, I understand; and you are wrong. I understand what you think because of tonight and because

I asked you in for a drink and then I came here. But that isn't why I came here, and I'm sorry you think that. I was frightened. That's why I came here. Even if I understand how you feel, I didn't expect it."

Packard saw that she wanted to cry but had decided not to and was fighting it. He was trying to push his own new distrust and dislike of her down. To think of her as a woman, in his room, in bed. It was harder than it should have been.

"Were you frightened because of what happened tonight, Sarah?"

"Because somebody was in my room tonight."

"When I took you home?"

"No. They weren't there then."

"Then how do you know it?"

"Because they took something."

"Did you tell the hotel people? Or the police?"

"No."

"Why didn't you?"

"I didn't want to; or I couldn't. I didn't want to."

Packard looked around at her suitcase and the briefcase.

"Did they take your typewriter? You had one on the helicopter."

"No. I left that with the elevator boy to prove I'd come back and pay my bill. I didn't want to wait. I'd have called the police about that."

"Then what did they take, Sarah?" His tone was softer, with interest and deliberate control.

"It doesn't make any difference. It was personal and not worth anything. But somebody went into the room when I was gone and went through my briefcase and took it. Then I knew we were followed tonight and it scared me silly and I came here, because there wasn't anyplace else. Now I'll get out as soon as I find me a room."

Packard said, "Lie down a minute and roll over."

Sarah stretched herself flat on the bed on her back and stared at the ceiling. She did not pull up the covers. Packard hung his slacks on the back of the arm chair with the belt and pockets toward the floor so that the weight pulled them flat. He got into the green and white bottoms of his striped pajamas. He walked around the bed and sat down on the edge of it beside Sarah.

"I'm sorry," he said again, still more gently. "I'm tired. I have a pain in my face. My brain quit working. Forgive me, Sarah."

He looked at her face, her breasts, the blue nylon twisted tight across her stomach, and he felt his want of her in the heat inside of him and his breathing. He knew he would be all right with her, whether he should or not.

"I'm glad somebody broke into your room."

"I was too, in a way, until I see how you've taken it."

"I know. I tried to explain. You try to forgive me. Tell me what they took."

"I wrote a letter that Mr. Farrel asked for. They took it."

"How did you happen to miss it?"

"It was in my briefcase. When we came home tonight, I found that the lock on the case was broken. So I went through it and the letter was gone."

"Nothing else?"

"No."

"What was in the letter?"

"Just a statement that Roger wanted me to make for promotion for the book. I wrote it and then I didn't mail it."

"Why not?"

"I didn't like the way it sounded. I wrote him another letter and told him so and said we could talk about it in Amsterdam."

"Did you sign the first letter?"

"Yes. Why?"

Packard was feeling his way, trying to learn what he could of the letter. But he listened as carefully to her voice for any indication that she was growing suspicious or resentful of his questions as he did for her answers.

"Just a question," he said.

But she lay there with a frown of concentration on her forehead, looking along the bed, past the foot of it, into space. She was thinking of herself and the things moving around her, and not of his right to question her.

"Why should anyone do it?" She was asking herself. "I could always write another one."

She said even more softly, "Roger wouldn't want the letter taken. I'm sure of that.

"You could write another one. If you still wanted to write it," Packard said. He took a chance. "Would the Russians want it taken?"

She looked sharply up at him, twisting her head to see his face, so that the muscles were tight on the side of her throat, as though she would be angry again. Then she looked down and shook her head.

"No, they wouldn't. The Russians wouldn't."

"Is that why you didn't send it?"

"I don't know. I'm not sure of anything now. I'm less sure after tonight," she said, not looking at him.

It was enough. It was all there would be for the time. Packard stood up and walked to the door. He turned off the overhead light and the floor lamp went off with it. The small orange bulb under a flowered shade on the table beside Sarah made the room smaller, the heavy furniture and sprawling shadows bigger. Street noises came up from the square below through the closed window and thick draperies at long intervals. The wind hit against the hotel in gusts, and Packard felt the cold in the room and touched the radiator. It had been turned off for the night.

He stood by the door and looked carefully around the room again, at the place of furniture and luggage and clothes, arranging these things in his mind. Then he went to the bed and got into it. Sarah had not moved.

"Will it be all right here?" she asked him. "I mean with the hotel people?"

"Yes; they don't care."

"Is it all right with you?"

"Everything is fine now. Turn out the light, Sarah."

She rolled onto her right side, pushed the button on the lamp. The first blackness of the room was absolute. Packard felt her beside him, on her back again, controlling her breathing, her body tight. The tenseness in her body and the waiting in it and the strangeness forced into his consciousness a picture of John's wife, kneeling beside the body, rigid under his touch, waiting to scream. He did not fight the picture or try to force it away.

Now it was time for him to think. John had put the letters where Packard could find them, where he would think to look for them. And where John could get them, too, if his scheduled meeting with Packard had come off. By morning Packard had to know where they were. He rolled onto his left side with the pillow against his chest and both arms around it.

"Sarah?"

"What, Packard?"

"Go to sleep now. It's late. You don't have to worry now."

"I wasn't worrying."

Packard could even laugh a little.

"All right," he said. "I'll talk to you about it tomorrow night. Go to sleep."

"How is your face?"

"Tired. Like all the rest of me. But better."

"That's good."

"Good night, Sarah."

"Good night."

She did not move. Packard began on the problem of the letters. He knew he had to start with places he and John had in common. John wanted him to have the letters. That was the key. The house? Already searched, torn apart by men trained for the job. Anything John had hidden there, he didn't want anybody to find.

78

Sarah shifted carefully on her side of the bed. The garden of the house? John hadn't expected him to have to dig up the flower beds. The Roi d'Espagne? Too far. Too hard. The same with Les Six Jeunes Hommes. How had John thought?

When he had finished talking to Packard on the telephone to the Six Jeunes Hommes, ready to leave for his meeting, he must have thought, If anything happens to me before I meet him, an accident, trouble, the letter has got to be where Packard will look for it.

Packard tried to force his mind to think. But it was slow and stubborn and the feel of Sarah next to him was a force and a desire, demanding, steady. He rolled onto his back and put the pillow above his head. Let the answer come in sleep if it would. He could not get it now. Not yet.

"Sarah?"

"Yes."

He turned on his right side, toward her. He felt for her head with his left hand and urged her very gently toward him. For an instant she was stiff under his touch. Then she turned quickly, with a sigh that was part groan, and put her mouth against his, open, soft with willingness and release.

Packard dropped his hand to her shoulder, then her breast, touching, holding, holding her tight then gently with his hand. She moved to him again, flattening her body against his, holding him against her with her hands behind his back, her breasts against him and her stomach and her thighs stretched against him. All Packard finally felt was the hungry, wanting heat, the heat of her against him. The heat of her inside him.

13

PACKARD woke her in the morning. He put one hand on her bare shoulder and shook her, awakening her with care.

"Hey," he said. "It's late."

She opened her eyes a little to the light, then opened them wide to see him. Then closed them again and held her arms up and out to him, and he dodged between them with his head and kissed her.

"Come on now," he said finally. "You have a plane to catch and a breakfast to eat and a bill to pay at the Atlanta. And you'd better get dressed too."

"I'd rather not."

"People will talk about you."

"They do anyway. How is your face?"

"You fixed it so that it doesn't hurt. Or I don't think about it. That's the same thing. How are you?"

"Oh, I'm good. I'm fine. If you'll call Sabena and get on the plane, I'll let go of you."

"All right."

Packard rolled across her to the little table beside her head. He picked up the telephone.

"If you do that again," she said, "we'll never get there."

Packard sat up on the edge of the bed. He told the operator in the lobby below that he wanted to speak to the Sabena ticket office. He waited, and Sarah got out of the bed and walked slowly around the room, getting ready.

"Good morning," a girl said at last on the telephone. "Sabena." Her voice was high and anxious to please.

"Good morning," Packard said in English. "You have a flight for Amsterdam at ten-five. Is that right?"

"Oh, yes, sir, that is right."

"Do you have one seat left on it for this morning?"

"Will you please wait one moment, sir? I will check."

Sarah came to stand beside him. She took her blue purse from the shelf of the little table, opened it and took out a cigarette and her lighter, and lit the cigarette. She twisted her head and blew the smoke back over her shoulder.

"Before breakfast?" Packard said. "There's a bad habit."

"Then I'll quit it."

"Just like that?"

"Just like that. Like Lent. For you."

She pushed the cigarette against an ash tray and left it with a thin line of smoke climbing from it.

"Hello, sir?" the Sabena girl said with the exaggerated politeness of airline people. "Thank you for waiting. I am sorry I was so long. Yes, sir, there is a seat on that plane. May I book you on it?"

"That is too bad," Packard said. "What is your next flight?"

"But sir, there is a seat."

"I understand. What about the next flight?"

"There is a Sabena flight leaving here at twelve-thirty arriving at Schiphol airport in Amsterdam at twenty minutes past one."

"Is there a seat on that one?"

"I will check it for you, sir. Please wait another moment."

Sarah looked over from the washbasin, her face dripping.

"Full?"

"Full."

"Damn it. Well come to the airport anyway. A seat always turns up."

"Hello, sir? Thank you for waiting again. I can also book you on the twelve-thirty if you prefer it."

"Good. No chance on the other one, though?"

"But certainly sir, as I said . . ."

"Well, then, twelve-thirty will be fine. How much is the ticket?"

She told him and Packard gave her his name.

"What time does the bus leave, and from where?"

"That isn't bad," he told Sarah when he had hung up. "I'll be there at one-thirty."

"That's all right. The other would be better."

"There is a waiting list. It will give you a chance to meet Farrel alone, and I'll see a little more of Brussels while I wait. Hurry up with that washbasin."

"You're in an awful rush to get out of here." It sounded as though she said that. She was brushing her teeth.

Packard was leaning over a suitcase.

"I'm having a moment of self-sufficiency," he told her. "Right now I can look at you as another piece of luggage to be gotten to the right plane on time."

She straightened up and looked back, holding the toothbrush, not sure enough of him to smile. She looked almost frightened.

"That's nice. How long do I stay a suitcase?"

"It could change at any second. So you'd better hurry."

She turned and looked into the wavy glass of the small mirror in its white wooden frame, smiling then, and combed her short dark hair quickly and did not answer him.

A blunt-nosed blue and white Sabena bus was parked ahead of their taxi at the downtown terminus. The driver in a gray uniform was loading the two last suitcases on the curb through a small door at the rear of it. A girl attendant with long dark hair and an overseas cap stood by the open front door of the bus with a clipboard in her hand. Packard waited until Sarah disappeared through the glass door of the building carrying her briefcase. A man in white overalls had her blue suitcase and the typewriter. The bus was full of people waiting to leave and they had nearly missed it.

"Now," Packard said to his taxi driver, "I would like to go for a ride. Toward Waterloo. Also along the Avenue Louise."

He got in and closed the door. The cab pulled away from the curb.

"Very well, monsieur. First to Waterloo?"

"First along the Avenue."

The day was cold and glaring bright and smelled clean. The wind had calmed and shifted to the north. A new wall of gray clouds had begun to build in that direction, but they were still far off. Packard sat back in the worn leather. Twice after they left the terminus he looked out of the rear window, studied the pattern of traffic in the street behind. Each time he turned back satisfied that he was not followed. The next place they could pick him up would be in the neighborhood of John's house. They might be watching that. They ought to be.

"Does Monsieur wish to see the Palace of the King?"

"Thanks, I've seen it."

Packard looked out the window on the right at the close joined gray brick buildings along the Boulevard, to the left at the bare-limbed trees on the parkway. He watched a bicycle rider grind his handlebars slowly left and right to keep his balance when they waited at a red light. He was less interested in a city in the daytime, and he knew where he was going and that was on his mind. He had known it at the instant he awoke, lying there beside Sarah. When the cab turned left into the Avenue Louise, Packard began to watch the street on both sides with care and to count the intersections and look down along them. The driver saw his interest through the mirror and slowed down.

At the end of the third block Packard said, "Where is the nearest telephone?"

"I do not know. In one of the shops perhaps. Or behind us, on the Boulevard."

"Is there no street booth closer?"

"I don't know, monsieur. Shall I go back?"

"No. There is no hurry, but if you see a booth, please stop."

John had said, "I ran all the way to the corner."

There were three cars in front of John's house when they passed it. There was a black Cadillac sedan with the CD license plates of the Corps Diplomatique, its chauffeur relaxed behind the wheel, reading. There was a gray Chevrolet sedan and a black one, both empty. So the American Ambassador was in the house with some of his official or unofficial family. If the Reds hadn't discovered before that those two Chevvies with their Belgian license plates were of interest to the Americans they knew it now. Packard shook his head.

People hurrying along the morning streets looked at the Cadillac as they went by, then up toward the house. Packard looked to the other side of the street. A man with no overcoat, wearing a beret pulled down on his forehead, walked slowly along reading a folded newspaper. He walked more slowly than the people on the street around him; too slow, on a day that was too cold for strolling and reading. He did not look toward the house or the cars, but he raised his eyes

82

as the taxi passed him going slowly. He stared closely then turned his head down and away toward his newspaper.

Before the next intersection Packard said, "Turn right at this corner, please."

The driver was midway through his turn when Packard saw the telephone booth. It was across the intersection, thirty feet off the Avenue Louise.

"And stop, please," he added. "There is a booth."

Packard got out and walked across the street to the booth. The taxi pulled ten yards farther down from the corner and parked, waiting. Through the frosted glass sides of the square booth Packard could see the dark solid of the telephone on one wall and he could see the distorted outline of a man's silhouette in front of the phone. The man's words came through the glass in broken garbled sounds like a bass Donald Duck. He was trying to talk someone into something, with determined patience.

Packard waited. The voice in the booth droned on, paused, laughed, began to talk again at once. Cars and bicycles passed going along the Avenue Louise and two boys down the block behind him were kicking a soccer ball and shouting. He looked across the Avenue Louise and saw the man with the beret and the newspaper come slowly along and stop at the corner, look casually back, toward John's house, while he refolded the paper. Packard moved to another side of the booth, putting it between him and the man in the beret.

He leaned against the glass and began to whistle so that the man inside would know that someone was waiting. The man tapped on the glass to silence him. Two women came down the flight of stone stairs in front of a red brick house down the street and stood at ease in the street and talked. Then one turned and came toward the booth. She walked directly to the door and opened it.

"Busy," the man inside shouted.

"Pardon," the woman said. She slammed the door.

Packard leaned around the corner. The man with the beret was looking down at his newspaper.

"Pardon, madame," Packard said. "But I also am waiting."

"You are not in front of the door."

"I am waiting out of the wind, but I have been here some time."

"My call is urgent."

"As is mine."

"But I, monsieur, am before the door."

She folded her arms across her chest and stood with them against the door of the booth. Packard looked away from her. The man on the Avenue Louise was staring at him across the scattered traffic, leaned forward. Then he straightened up.

83

He let the newspaper drop to the sidewalk where the wind caught it and opened it and sifted it away in large, slow-turning sections. The man took off his beret and held it up while he ran his other hand across his hair. The signaling was obvious. Packard stepped into the street and looked in four directions, but the building cut off his view out along the Avenue Louise.

He stepped back and reached beside the woman. He took the handle of the booth door and pulled.

"No!" The woman shouted. She put her head down and leaned against the door.

Packard heaved and the door opened, pushing the woman away. He stepped into the booth. The small man inside turned with angry surprise and waved his hand up and down at Packard to go away.

"One moment," he said into the telephone.

The instrument hung on the wall opposite the door. A single shelf below it had a thick telephone book on a chain that went from a metal plate on the back of the book to a heavy bolt through the shelf. Nothing else in the booth. The man had dropped the handpiece of the telephone so that it swung on its rubber cord like a pendulum. He was pushing against Packard's chest with both hands and yelling. The woman outside had braced her feet on the wood of the sill and was pulling on his coat.

Packard turned sideways and wedged the small man into the corner with his hip and held him. He slapped the woman's hands from his clothing. He picked up the telephone book and held the open edges down and shook it. He looked inside both covers and dropped it back on the shelf. The woman was outside the booth now, screaming at her friend.

"Edna! Edna!"

The small man had caught the swinging telephone and clutched it to his chest like a baby in danger. Packard ran his hand underneath the shelf, halfway, until it struck against paper. He pulled and felt the gum give and the envelope come loose in his hand. He stuffed the envelope into the pocket of his topcoat and felt the rest of the way under the shelf. Nothing more. He turned and ran out of the phone booth toward the taxi.

The driver had gotten out to see the action in the telephone booth and was standing beside his cab. He stood there as Packard came across the street.

"Quickly!" Packard called. "Let's go!"

The driver hesitated, frowning, thinking of the possibility of the police and trouble. Packard pulled open the back door.

"Quickly," he said again, hard.

The driver got into the cab and started the motor. Packard

84

looked out the rear window. The man in the beret was standing on the other side of the Avenue Louise pointing at him. A blue German Opel sedan was stalled in the middle of a left turn in the intersection by a line of cars going past. Packard saw only two men, in the front seat, then his taxi swung into the street and started off.

"Take me to the central post office. And if you want money from me do not let us be caught by the blue automobile behind."

Packard looked back once more as the driver cut close to the curb in a right-hand turn. The blue Opel was there and closing on the ancient taxi. Packard sat back in the left corner of the back seat, out of line of the window. He twisted around and pulled the envelope out of his pocket and sat back and looked at it. It was a plain white business envelope without writing, only the blob of hardening chewing gum, stretched and stringy, which had held it to the shelf in the phone booth.

He tore it across the top and pulled out the letter. It was on white bond, dated in mid-October, which Sarah had addressed to Farrel and had signed. Stapled to it was a short note, also to Farrel, a carbon copy of a letter, on flimsy yellow paper, unsigned and dated later than the other. He read the longer letter.

Dear Mr. Farrel:
This is my first opportunity since the rush of departure to thank you for all you have done for me, and particularly for your confidence in me at a time when older friends have stayed away since the witch-hunters drove me out of my work.

I welcome this chance to finish a task that I have wanted to do since my first visit to Russia. It is high time to give our country an honest and understanding picture of that great and courageous people who were once our allies and who are working peacefully to fulfill a destiny which no selfish system and its threats can deny them. I hope to be able to paint such an honest portrait.

If this book is finished as I wish it, your enlightenment and generosity and, most important, your bravery in sponsoring my work will be directly responsible. For to stay now and work in America where the writer is permitted to take his nourishment only from the troughs filled by businessmen and the government that serves them would be dishonorable and destructive even if it were possible. When the owners of the Carter newspapers can be frightened into firing me, when my friends and associates can be terrified into avoiding me so that they can continue to eat and feed their families, then the climate of the mind is barren desert and Freedom of Speech is a dull chant set in propaganda rhythms.

I thank you again for the chance you have given me to escape. And I can tell you that if I find in Russia even a part of the vigorous, dedicated leadership that I remember, even a fraction of the selfless devotion of a people to each other and their motherland, even some of the longing for honorable peace, for a chance to construct rather than destroy, and willingness to recognize and reward the merits of the individual for his part in the whole, I will stay there, if they will let me, where I can write the truth and send it out to those few ears at home which are not closed, into those few minds which are not petrified with fear.

For whatever success comes of these bright hopes, I have you to thank and I do thank you.

SARAH BORSEN

The second letter was very brief:

Dear Mr. Farrel:

In reply to your note, I did write the letter which you keep asking for and included in it many of the points we have discussed, even the details of my feelings at this time and the plan which I have considered to stay abroad and write, as you suggested I should. But the next morning I did not like the sound of it, and I think it might well do the book more harm than good. Since we are now to meet in Holland, I will carry it with me as it is and we can discuss it there.

SARAH

Packard's face reflected angry disgust as he read the letter over, concentrating on it until he knew what was in it. Then he glanced at the carbon again, and held both papers in his lap.

Well, that was lush enough! But she hadn't mailed it, and that was a point for her anyway. A small one. If she had written and talked at home as she did in the letter, he ought to help her get to Russia, not try to hold her back. Still, if she had changed her mind.

He folded the papers together and put them in the inside pocket of his sports coat, balancing against a sudden lurch of the taxi. He glanced around at the Opel, getting closer, and shifted back into the corner of the seat and shook his head.

It didn't make sense yet. Who was in the car behind him? Who had worked on John? Sarah was right about one thing: The Russians wouldn't want to steal the letter or to keep her from making it public. There was nothing in it to make a government kill for it. Except his own government. They could want it. That much?

And Farrel? All Farrel had to do was wait and she would hand it to him. Even if she didn't, it wouldn't help him or the Russians to get rough about it. Sarah was a nice potential propaganda chance, not an international spy with the defense secrets.

What they had told him about her didn't make her big

86

enough for what was going on. But Farrel had asked for the letter, and kept asking for it. She said that in the carbon. They had left her alone last night and this morning as long as the letter was missing. They needed the letter first, it looked like, and Farrel had asked for it. Whatever was cooking, Farrel looked like the man at the stove. For someone. Maybe for himself; but someone was furnishing him with a lot of support.

Packard gave it up and looked behind. The blue sedan was there, its bumpers almost touching the taxi. They were near the center of the old town and the traffic was heavy and confused with pedestrians and bicycle riders and Belgian drivers who were not good. He could see the man beside the driver, leaning forward, poised to jump out if the taxi had to stop.

"The car is very close," Packard said to the driver.

He shrugged.

"There is traffic," he said. "And the police."

"I know. The car behind carries more danger than both."

"To you perhaps, monsieur."

Packard smiled.

"There is that," he said. "How far is the post office?"

"Three minutes more. Five minutes."

Packard looked back again. He took a pen from his pocket and wrote the license number of the Opel on a corner of the empty envelope and tore it off and dropped it beside the driver.

"Should there be an accident, that might help the police."

A policeman held up one arm sharply to stop them at an intersection. The driver slowed and shifted down to first gear. Cars and bicycles began to move in on him from each side. Then he went through the cross street. The policeman blew his whistle in short startled blasts. He stepped out of the center of the street in their direction, reaching for his pencil and notebook. He had to jump back out of the way of the blue sedan as it charged through after them. The driver of a bug-sized Fiat had taken advantage of the second's interval to turn right and swing in behind their taxi, in front of the Opel.

Packard watched the Fiat driver behind him looking back over his shoulder at the Opel, righteously angry that it had gone through a stop, refusing to let it pass, slowing down obstinately to obstruct it. Packard could hear the screeching, demanding bleats of the police whistle along the whole block, bouncing off the high bricks of the houses in the narrow street.

"Good. Well done. Now get ahead as far as you can. How far?"

"Very near, monsieur. Two turns more."

They made one turn, beside a gray building with the high peaked roof of a theater or an opera house. The Fiat behind followed stubbornly. The blue Opel swung to pass it, honking, failed, fell back. They turned left again and stopped abruptly at the curb before the dirty stone face of the post office. The Fiat driver continued straight ahead when they turned and the Opel swung around the corner, aimed for the curb. Packard dropped a fold of bills beside the driver and ran for the entrance in a crooked line, up the steps, and in through the doors.

Along one wall he saw an open window, brass barred, without a line, and made for it. An old man with white hair in a blue coat with official brass buttons sat behind the bars, counting stamps from one pile into another.

"Please," Packard said. "I want an envelope."

He pulled Sarah's letter from his coat.

"And I want stamps enough to send this airmail to America."

He put fifty francs on the ledge.

The old man continued counting.

"One moment," he said.

"Please," Packard said. "Please. Now!"

"You are an American?" The old man did not look up.

"Yes."

"Do Americans never have time?"

"Please!"

"Very well. Very well, monsieur."

Packard took his pen out of his pocket and looked over his shoulder. A heavy man, middle-aged, in a tight brown overcoat with a narrow-brimmed hat set squarely on the middle of his head was standing there, still holding the door open with one hand, looking along the cages. He had the other hand in the pocket of his overcoat. Packard turned back to the window. It was the flat-faced man. The man who had come into Sarah's hotel with Rosy Cheeks the night before. The old man had selected an envelope from an open drawer and pushed it forward. It was too small. Packard folded the letter once, down the middle. He forced it into the envelope and licked the flap and sealed it, rubbing the flap with his fist. He had his pen open and he addressed the envelope to Mrs. P. S. Gray at the Washington address which did exist. He wrote "Air Mail" in the top middle of the envelope and pushed it back to the old man, behind the protection of the grill.

"Now the stamps," he said, and felt the hard shove of metal in his back, low, just below the kidneys, where a man's gun would be if he had his hand in the pocket of his overcoat.

"You said airmail?"

"Yes."

"Get the letter back. Give it to me," Flat Face said in French.

The voice was rough as though he needed to clear his throat and it was louder than a whisper. Packard always felt his emotions in the stomach. He felt the slight sick cramp there now. The old man looked up from tearing off the stamps.

"What did you say?"

"Nothing, it was this man."

Packard nodded back with his head. He put both of his hands on the wooden counter and leaned back into the gun.

"There you are."

The old man dropped the envelope face down onto the counter. He put one stamp down on it with one hand, another down on it with the other.

"Now give me the letter!" The barrel of the gun jabbed.

The old man looked up with the fifty francs in his hand.

"Pardon?"

"It was the man behind me."

"Is he with you?"

"No."

The old man looked around Packard's shoulder.

"Monsieur," he said, "I am doing business with this gentleman. You will please wait. Or use another window."

His high old voice was sharp and firm, with the power of the government post in it. He looked back to Packard and held up the bill.

"This is just correct, monsieur."

"Will you put the stamps on for me?" Packard said. "I cannot use my fingers well."

"You wrote with them."

"But now they are cramped again. The war."

"Ah! The war!"

"I give you one chance more. The letter." The shove of the gun hurt all the way down to Packard's groin.

"Pardon?"

"The man behind me."

The old man licked one stamp and put it in place. Then he licked the other and put it neatly beside the first. Packard felt the pressure of the gun release. He sensed the shift of weight. The man was going to grab. Packard pushed away another inch from the counter, making his own weight ready.

The old man reached up with one hand and slammed the gate of the cage into place. He glared past Packard's right shoulder.

"This window is now closed," he said.

He reached his right hand behind him without looking and dropped the letter into a cardboard box.

"Thank you, monsieur," Packard said. He let his hands drop to his sides.

"It goes without saying."

Packard turned around very slowly and looked into the round, flat, cold face staring at him. He felt his own heart beating slowly and heavily.

"I will remember you," he said, his voice so low that it did not carry in the vast room. "This man will remember you." He nodded back at the old man in the window, counting stamps again. "The policeman will remember your car. You cannot use a gun in a place like this and go free. Which I knew, too. You are not good in your job. I think you are through here. Especially because I will remember you and last night. And so will my people."

He took a step toward the man. Another against him, until the heavy man moved back a pace, then Packard walked past him and across the lobby and out the door. He waited on the sidewalk, among the people passing, until the man came out of the gray building and got into the Opel. Then Packard turned left and crossed the street at the corner, then left again along the Rue Fosse aux Loups until he could stop a cab. He rode in it to the Place Rogier and got out close to the old Gare du Nord and walked slowly back toward the Cosmopolite, watching the patterns of the street and the cars carefully. When he felt sure he was not followed, he went into the hotel and up to his room.

After he had finished packing he sat down at the desk and took a small black notebook out of his pocket and made a complete list on one of the pages of the money he had spent on dinner the night before, on taxicabs in Brussels, on the cost of his trip to Brussels and the price of his flight to Amsterdam. He would have to certify to these charges on his expense account. He thought and remembered so as to make them carefully correct. He always had the feeling that expense accounts were a lurking trap, a trap that had been set for someone else, but one that he might fall into.

14

AT THE American Express office in Amsterdam, Packard asked for his mail and smiled openly when the clerk handed him the envelope. It was a rich lavender, addressed in Kelly green ink. Lois was a girl of passion. He talked to another clerk about hotel reservations. The clerk went to a telephone and when he came back he wrote the name Pays-Bas on a slip of paper, and an address.

"It is not the season, sir," he said. "There is a room. The hotel is very good and close to the Hotel de l'Europe. But less expensive. It is not a long walk. Or you can ride in a taxi. You are an American?"

"Yes."

"There will be a taxi just in front."

"I think I'll walk."

The clerk gave him instructions and a small folder map of the city. Packard carried his suitcases to another counter. A girl was sitting behind it adding a column of figures on a ruled pad.

"Will you get me the American Embassy in The Hague, please?" Packard said.

"Go into booth number 2," the girl said. She did not look up.

Packard waited in the booth with the bad sweet smell of stale tobacco. He looked at the numbers scratched on the plaster wall and wondered what the conversation would be like if he called one. He looked at his suitcases through the window. Someone had plastered a "Hotel Cosmopolite—Brussels" sticker on each one. He'd have to scrape them. Finally a girl at the American Embassy answered the phone.

"May I speak with Ralph Dickson," he said.

"One moment, please."

A pause. Another girl.

"Mr. Dickson's office."

"May I speak with Mr. Dickson, please."

"Who may I tell Mr. Dickson is calling, sir?"

"Peter Stuyvesant."

"Thank you, Mr. Stuyvesant. One moment, please."

Next a young man's voice.

"Ralph Dickson, Mr. Stuyvesant."

"Mr. Dickson, this is Packard Gray. I'm in Amsterdam. I just got in from Brussels."

"Oh. Mr. Gray. Well, we've wondered where you'd gotten to. Can you come in here?"

"Not very well, Mr. Dickson. I don't have a car. And I have a date shortly. I'm going to stay at the Hotel Pays-Bas. Can you meet me there?"

"Well, let me see. It's two-fifteen. You're about thirty-five miles over there. Well, I suppose I could. What happened in Brussels with the Borsen girl?"

"That's fine, Mr. Dickson. I'll be in my room anytime after three. I'll see you then."

"Oh. Well, all right. Goodbye, Mr. Gray."

91

"Goodbye."

Outside the afternoon was dark. A cold wet wind came across the waters of the canals and the heavy clouds were low. It was going to rain. Or snow. Packard walked along with his suitcases, keeping a canal to his left. The water was black and oily, calm even in the wind because of the high walls beside it. Low barges bulging and turned up at the ends hung to banks by thick ropes. High, narrow houses were on his right. The air smelled of wetness and the sea and creosote, and a winter city in midafternoon.

At last Packard came to a bridge across the canal on his right. He put the bags down to rest his arms and stood and watched a boy and a girl come off the bridge toward him on two bicycles, their arms around each other as they rode. He turned right down a narrow streetway and in the middle of that block, on his right, came to the Hotel Pays-Bas, the two steps to its entrance sheltered by a narrow overhang.

There was a drawing room on his right filled with heavy red-brown furniture and solid flat reading tables. It had a musty feel like an old, fine club gone downhill, and it was empty. Beyond it a wide carpeted staircase led to the floors above. Straight ahead of the entrance was a small bar, empty too, except for a man and woman in brown unpressed tweeds sitting at a table. They looked like English tourists waiting for the rain so they could take a walk. The desk was on his left.

They gave Packard a room on the first floor above the lobby. He climbed up to it with the bellboy ahead of him carrying the suitcases. The first landing was a small window-less mezzanine with a writing desk, a couch and two over-stuffed high-backed red chairs. They turned right off the stairs and went along a dark hall, jogged once to the left and stopped in front of a door next to a window that was open with the curtains bulging inward on the cold wind. Twenty feet beyond, the hall ended in a door that was open. Packard could see the old chipped bathtub with clawed feet on balls. Then the bellboy got the door unlocked and waited for Packard to go into a room that was small and cold and dim because the draperies were drawn tight across the windows.

The bellboy put both bags on a wood stand with canvas cross straps and opened the curtains. He turned the valve on a radiator that clanked and hissed when the water flowed into it, then he waited by the door and Packard tipped him with two German marks.

"Is that all right?" he asked again.

"Thank you, sir. The toilet is just to your left in the hall.

The second door on the right side. The bathroom is at the end of the hall."

"Thank you."

The boy took the key out of the door and put it on the green blotter of the desk and went out and closed the door. Packard looked out of the window into the hollow gray court of the hotel. He opened the wardrobe door to begin his check of the room. Then he closed the door without looking and sat down in a fat armchair facing the door and took the letter from Lois out of his pocket and tore the end from it.

Dearest Packie:

Welcome to Amsterdam. But I am only sorry that I could not have met you. Daddy is not well and so long as he is not I will have to neglect you, knowing you will understand and forgive.

We were all interested and astonished by the story of your recent adventures, and I hope that you will write me a full account at your earliest opportunity. I know that you will soon see our stately mutual friend, and selfish girl that I am, I would like you to write me the news first because I would be jealous of having to hear such a story secondhand.

You are such a wanderer that I am sure you did not hear that we have moved and therefore the old address will no longer reach us. As soon as I hear that you have gotten my little letter and are settled I will send you the new address. But daddy is so ill and must have such quiet that for the time being I don't want anyone but you to know where to reach us and bother daddy with upsetting if well-meant sympathies.

And so goodbye for now. We are anxious to hear from you and hope that your stay here will be all that can be wished. With the same warmest affection.

LOIS

Authenticated. Clear. He did have an assistant. Someone that Nick would put close but leave unidentified. OSA in Amsterdam already knew of the trouble in Brussels and wanted his immediate, detailed report on it. They did not want him to give the story of John to State through Mr. Dickson. The mail channel from Lois by American Express was closed, but a new one would reopen for him so that he could submit his report and make contact as soon as Dickson told them where he was and that he had received the Lois letter.

If they were closing the American Express channel they believed he had been known in Brussels or would be immediately and his mail was not safe there. The warnings of daddy's sickness were repeated. They were telling him not to lead the opposition home, to keep American interests covered. He had failed to alert John. He had a sermon coming.

He got up out of the chair and took a book of matches from the thin slit lips of a black ceramic ash tray on the desk. He walked out into the hall and went into the toilet where he set fire to the letter and the envelope and held them until he burned his fingers, then he dropped the ashes into the toilet and pulled the wooden knob on the chain that came down from a water box. He watched while the black bits rolled and then whirled and spun out of the bottom of the bowl. Then he went back past his room and along the hall and down the staircase to the desk.

"I just checked in," he reminded the very proper, formal clerk.

"Yes, Mr. Gray, of course. Is something the matter?"

"I wondered if you have another single room without a bath?"

"Is there something wrong with the room?"

"No. Not with the room. Only I would like not to be on the court. It's dark, and I would rather look out on the street if I can."

"It is not so quiet above the street."

"I know. I like the city noise."

"There is nothing on the street on the first floor."

"I do not mind the second or the third."

"One moment, Mr. Gray. I will see."

He turned to a counter behind him and looked at the open pages of a large ledger book, bound in green cloth with a red leather trim showing at the bottom. He moved his thin finger down the page and stopped it. He looked up toward the key boxes and turned back to Packard. He motioned to a bellboy, and spoke to him in Dutch.

"He will change your luggage to room 358. It is above the street. I hope you will like it, but it is not so close to the bath."

"That's all right. I'm sure it will be fine. Thank you."

"And here is your passport, Mr. Gray. We are done with it."

The bellboy went off to get the luggage. Packard climbed on, directly to 358, and leaned against the cream-colored door of the room and waited. He was in Amsterdam, on Wednesday, in the middle of a November afternoon that was dark with clouds and the threat of rain or snow. It was a dark time. There had been one murder. The city was strange. It was not the time to take favors. Not the first room offered you, especially if the clerk pointed out its advantages.

It was a dark time and a strange city and he had come to it without cover because when he picked up the letters from the phone booth in Brussels he had taken an open hand in the action and someone here would already know it. He knew that someone here knew it and he knew which side they were on and that was all. They knew who he was. He did not know them. It was not the time to take the first room or the hand of a stranger or count any man a friend.

Packard heard the bellboy puffing up the stairs and thought of ghosts and smiled. You saw ghosts when you began to suspect that the desk clerk and the bellboy and the organ grinder and the bartender were each an enemy agent. You were in bad shape when you saw too many ghosts. You were in worse shape when you missed one.

When the bellboy had come and gone Packard locked the door and pulled the draperies shut again and went over the room as he had in Brussels. The fixtures, the wires, the electric outlets. When he had finished, he opened the draperies and he took a pad of stationery out of one of his suitcases and sat down at the desk in front of the windows. For a minute or two he listened to the traffic in the street below him, while he looked across the space of the street to an office building opposite where he could see two girls, one in a light tan blouse, one in a dark brown sweater; both chunky, with short brown hair and neither one was pretty. The one in the blouse was delivering papers from a pile in her arms onto the desks. The other was stopping at each desk to pick up papers and carry them away. Packard nodded understandingly. If it was a government office, they were probably the same papers. He took his pen from his pocket and pulled the wooden chair close to the desk and began to write out the report that Lois was waiting for. He began with Bonn.

15

WHEN the telephone rang Packard looked at his watch. Three-thirty. He folded the cover shut on the pages he had written and got up and answered the telephone, sitting on the edge of his bed.

"Mr. Gray."

"Yes."

"There is a Mr. Dickson in the lobby, sir."

"Fine. Ask him to come up, will you?"

"Yes, sir. Thank you, sir."

Packard went to the desk. He opened the pad and put the

pages of his report in order and closed the pad and put it back into the suitcase. Dickson had made good time, but he could have done better than give his name at the desk. It made a sure link with American interests. It could make one. But then Dickson didn't spend his life thinking what each of his movements could mean to the one who watched him. Or even that someone might watch him. It was the risk you ran working with amateurs. Packard waited until he heard the knock before he opened the door.

"Mr. Gray?"

Packard said, "Come in."

"I'm Ralph Dickson, Mr. Gray."

They shook hands. Mr. Dickson was not very young. But he dressed to look young. He wore a very dark flannel suit and a black knit tie. His shoes were black loafers cut in the Italian style, low and pointed, with small leather tassels. He had a narrow-brimmed dark brown felt hat with a dark blue band which he dropped on the bed, and no overcoat. He had a thin pale face and narrow slightly rounded shoulders, made narrower by the straight cut of his suit. Mr. Dickson had the look of a well-preserved bachelor instructor in English Literature at a proper New England preparatory school. Good at Gilbert and Sullivan roles, and popular with faculty wives.

"Sit down, Mr. Dickson," Packard said. He pointed to the cushioned chair with wooden arms to the left of the desk, out of line of the window.

"Thank you."

Packard swung the wooden desk chair around to face him.

"Is this your usual weather for November?" he asked.

"Pretty normal," Mr. Dickson said. "We go under the clouds in October and manage to come out again, if we're lucky, in April."

"In time for the tulips, eh?"

"And the tourists. It's all very well worked out."

Mr. Dickson took a pack of cigarettes from his pocket and offered one to Packard, then lit one himself and dropped the match in the wastebasket beside him.

"How did you come up?" he asked. "Fly?"

"Yes."

"Was it rough?"

"It was a little rough before we landed, in the clouds. The rest was fine."

"I like to stay on the ground in the winter if I can. Of course when the Old Man says 'fly,' I fly."

His tone implied that there were those times when the Old Man called him in and said, "Dickson, I need you in Istanbul by evening."

"I guess we all do."

"Well, what do you have to tell me, Mr. Gray?"

"I was told to call you as soon as I got here. What do you want to know?"

Mr. Dickson punched his cigarette out against the painted inside of the wastebasket, a shower of small sparks tumbling from the end.

"Well, now, as I understand it," he said briskly, "your job is to help us keep the Borsen girl from embarrassing the United States government. I'm to report on your progress with this to the Old Man himself."

"Who is the Old Man?"

"Well, we call him that. The Ambassador."

"I see. You'll forgive me, Mr. Dickson, but do you have any official identification with you?"

"Why, yes."

Mr. Dickson took a pale pigskin billfold from the inside pocket of his suitcoat and spread it open. He took a laminated oblong identity card from one of the several pockets and handed it across to Packard. Packard looked at it closely. He handed it back.

"Thanks. You understand, I hope, that I didn't really think you could be anything at all but what you claim to be." He said it very seriously.

"Oh, I understand. After all you've never seen me before."

"No." Packard took his passport out of his coat pocket, "And you haven't seen me before."

Mr. Dickson glanced inside the green book and handed it back. He looked around the room. Packard watched him beginning to enjoy the picture of himself as a spy. He took another cigarette out of his shirt pocket and lighted it.

"Now," he said. "What about the Borsen girl?"

"Yes, the Borsen girl. I met her on the flight from Bonn yesterday as directed. I spent the evening with her in Brussels last night. I took her to the Sabena bus this morning. She is going to meet her publisher friend, Farrel, here. She's living at the Hotel de l'Europe, and I will get in touch with her again as soon as we finish here."

"Is she still going back into Russia?"

"So far as I know she hasn't changed her plans yet. She might be a little less certain."

"Then we still have the problem."

"After twelve or so full hours you still have the problem."

"Have you talked it out with her?"

"I spent most of the time just getting acquainted."

Mr. Dickson hitched his chair to the left. He slumped down in it and crossed his ankles, with his feet propped on the edge of the desk. He hooked his thumbs under his chin and put his two index fingers lightly over his lips. He was considering the problem. Smoke wobbled upward from his cigarette.

"It seems to me that you ought to be able to point out to her how much damage she can do herself and her country if she goes on this way. A lot of these fuzzy-thinking radicals can be jostled back into line by words like 'treason' or 'dishonor.' She's flirting with both if she goes off asking the Russians for asylum, you know."

"I'm sure other people have talked to her, Mr. Dickson, before now. But she's been on a peace crusade, and she still is. If she plans to run off, it will be to punish us because we haven't appreciated her for trying to save us. Like a suicide who wants everyone to miss him when he's gone. As I said, though, I think she has some new doubts."

"Well, I can't help feeling all the time that this is more of a case of ideological orientation that the Department could have laid on in Washington, rather than a job for you chaps. After all, she's not unintelligent."

"I imagine our chaps would have been happy for your chaps to handle it," Packard said, irritated. "I would. I don't like this way of doing things. I don't think it's an OSA job to straighten out people with unpopular political ideas. As long as they are only unpopular. As far as anyone has told me, hers are."

Mr. Dickson took his hands down from his face and pointed his cigarette at Packard.

"Because of Miss Borsen's fame, Mr. Gray," he said, "the Department considers this an exceptional case. A matter of great importance."

"I agree with them," Packard told him, "but my reasons are different. Would you chaps like to take it over?"

Mr. Dickson looked shocked and annoyed. As though he had to explain politely to a distant relative why he was not going to be able to loan him a large sum of money.

"Unfortunately in a time of investigating committees and peace overtures we aren't allowed much going off into the market place to work with our hands. Just the matter of Policy takes up our time and effort at home and abroad."

"I see," Packard said. "Well, let's get on with it. There are one or two other things for you to report. We were followed last night in Brussels. And somebody went into her room and stole a letter from her briefcase. She had written it to Farrel, the man who is going to publish her book. He's up here now. Do you know anything about him?"

"No. Good Lord. And everything has been running like clockwork up here. Relations have never been better. I hope this thing isn't going to kick over the bucket and spill ashes all over our floor."

Packard got impatient. Dickson's pat, automatic jargon irritated him. Dickson's official self-protective reaction to his report disgusted him.

"I can see what a nuisance it is for you," he said, "but I think there will be trouble. There already is. She's up here with her bags packed, ready to leave, and you haven't issued her any permits. She wrote a letter to Farrel and then decided not to send it. Last night they followed us all over Brussels until that letter was stolen from her. Then they quit following us. The letter was strongly favorable to the Russians, Mr. Dickson, and just as critical of us."

Dickson looked at him suspiciously.

"You fellows didn't take it, did you?" he asked.

"Ah," Packard said slowly, losing the edge of his antagonism to Dickson in thinking. "You ask that, too!"

"Why not? Our request specifically instructed . . ."

"It's odd. It's odd because we're the ones who should have taken it. Everybody would believe that we're the only ones who would want it. I thought so myself.

"Ah," he said, still more slowly.

It came up from below his consciousness, in bits at first, and it was clear to him and he did not doubt it because it was all that made sense.

His body stiffened involuntarily because he had had an instant's urge to get up from the chair and leave Dickson and his fussing talk and find Sarah quickly. But he was not through with Dickson, so he sat there and began to talk again, but faster now, under pressure.

"Now I think there will be big trouble," he repeated. "You asked if we took the letter. Sarah wonders if the Americans took it. Even I couldn't see why anyone else would want it. Because for propaganda it would hurt us so much. And only us."

"Well," Dickson said scornfully, but without great concern, "that's typical of her kind. After all the nasty things she's said for publication. Why bother to steal the thing, though?"

He shrugged and slouched back in the chair.

"It's just typical of her," he repeated. Then he looked suspicious again. "How do you know so much about what was in it?" he demanded.

"Because she told me."

"Well. You did get acquainted, didn't you.".

Packard let it go by. "The letter," he said, "told what a great place Russia is, and that if she got in there she'd stay and work for . . ."

"Which is just what we are afraid of, Mr. Gray. And that's why we asked you to . . ."

"And she had signed the letter, too. So there will be no doubt that it's authentic. Now suppose someone gets the letter and something happens to Sarah Borsen?"

"Something happens to her? What happens to her?"

Packard was trying to explain it to Dickson, and think it through, as he went.

"Somebody kills her. What will it look like? Just wait a minute, Mr. Dickson. Let me finish it. The letter is stolen and Sarah is killed and then the letter gets to the press."

He paused.

"Maybe through Farrel's newspapers."

That must be it. That would explain the generous Mr. Farrel and why he wanted the letter from Sarah. You *could* explain it that way.

Dickson was staring at him.

"It will look as if we killed her ourselves, Mr. Dickson."

Dickson smiled nervously.

"Everyone knows we don't do business that way," he said uneasily.

"Don't we? You asked us to work on her, didn't you? Once you start it, it's hard to stop. If this thing happens to Sarah, people who never would have believed it before will think that Uncle Sam killed off one of his own people—a famous one, who was going to expose him and make him look bad and ask the Russians for help. You can see how they'd believe it, don't you, Mr. Dickson?"

Mr. Dickson sat silent, thinking about it. Packard looked away, out the window at the darkening sky.

"And they'll have evidence in her signed letter. That's the kind of trouble I think I've got, Mr. Dickson," Packard said.

He heard Dickson shift upright in his chair, and did not turn his eyes. Dickson's feet hit the floor with a heavy sound in the quiet room.

"But, my God!" he said in a coarse, dramatic whisper as though he was for the first time unsure; afraid he was overheard. "They already have the letter."

Packard shook his head.

"I don't think so. But I'll bet they try to get another."

"Then who does have it?"

"I don't know who has it right now. But the Russians don't."

"Gray!"

"What?"

"Is this tied up with that murder in Brussels?"

"What murder in Brussels?"

"It's in every paper. An American named Anderson was killed there last night. The papers said it was a robbery."

Packard said easily, "I haven't read the papers. But I never knew anyone there named Anderson."

"By God we'd better not be mixed up in it. Why, this is getting to be a terrible thing. I know the Department and the Old Man didn't expect anything like this at all. What's going to happen to relations up here?"

Packard thought of John with his pipe, big and alive in the Roi d'Espagne, and on the floor in the middle of his own living room, tumbled over, chained to a chair dead. And of Sarah who did not know her danger. He looked at the righteous face of this old young man, sitting back now in his chair, lighting another cigarette, speaking for the Department of State of the United States Government.

"If you are afraid of my disturbing the local situation," he said, "then have your Ambassador contact Washington. I take my orders from there. But my leaving won't change the kind of trouble you've got, or save the girl."

"It isn't a question of fear, Mr. Gray." Mr. Dickson's feelings were hurt. "Our position in protecting American interests is necessarily one of caution and of balancing values. The force of an incident here must be carefully weighed for its effect on the entire domestic and foreign attitudes."

"Weigh this one," Packard said. "You'll find it's a honey."

Mr. Dickson ground out the cigarette he had just lighted. He looked out the window.

"You know," he said unhappily after a moment, "we get all the blame."

"Yes," Packard admitted. "I know you do."

They sat for a few seconds while the darkness of the room increased. Then Packard shook himself out of his thoughts and the unpleasantness of the mood the conversation had left.

"Are you in touch with any of my people?" he asked.

"There is a man at the Embassy for liaison. I'm to brief him along with the Ambassador."

"Well, tell him, will you, that I'd like a gun. A .38 Colt Detective Special if he has one on hand. Or better still that lightweight one. They call it a Cobra. And a shoulder holster."

"Do you really expect to need that?"

"I'd like to have it. Just tell him. Do you remember all we've said?"

Mr. Dickson got up. Packard stood and pushed his chair back under the desk and waited while Dickson walked past, looking at him sideways as though he were slightly afraid.

101

"Yes. I have a good memory anyway."

Mr. Dickson picked up his hat.

"This will be quite a shocker at the building. I suppose I'd better count on coming by tomorrow to see you."

"No, I think it's better if you don't come here at all again. Being seen with you would make a direct link between me and our Embassy. I don't want that to happen."

"Then how do we keep in touch with you?"

"I'll call you, from a public telephone, if I have something to report. Don't call me here. It goes through a switchboard. When I call I'll use the name of Peter. Otherwise I'm not the caller. You've already given your name downstairs. Someone might get it and call, using my name, to see what your reaction will be when you answer the phone. See whether we knew each other, how well, or that kind of thing. You understand?"

"Sure. Do you think they will?"

"I hope not. I hope they don't know where I am yet. One more thing. Just in case. It's four-twenty. Do you have to go back to your office?"

"No. I don't have to. Can I take you somewhere?"

"No. Where is your car?"

"Back at the end of the block. Across the street from the Doelen Hotel."

"Leave it there and go back to The Hague on a train or bus tonight. Have someone else pick it up tomorrow, and park it in a garage in The Hague. Do you have a friend who doesn't work at the Embassy that you could spend the night with?"

Mr. Dickson looked very surprised and a red flush spread over his smooth face.

"Well, yes. I think so."

"It could be a male friend, too," Packard said dryly. "When you leave here, go to your friend and spend the night and go from there to work in the morning. Then don't go back to your friend's house for three or four days at least. Can you do that?"

"It's all pretty inconvenient. Are you sure all this cloak-and-dagger business is essential to the picture?"

Packard looked at him, surprised, wondering if the whole afternoon's conversation had made any impression on him at all.

"I'm already known," he said, forcing himself to patience. "If they are watching me, you may be followed. I'm trying to get you out of here without anybody being able to tell where you live or where you work. If we're lucky this may do it. If not, too bad; we don't have time for the advanced course."

102

side to throbbing and sweat was standing out on his face and he was sick in his stomach. When he slid the gun into the holster it rubbed just across the bandages of the knife wound and he took it off and shoved it into his suitcase and put on his blue suitcoat and dropped the gun into the right-hand pocket.

He put three of the extra shells into each of his trouser pockets and sprinkled the other six into his open suitcase. He looked at his watch. Five minutes before one. But his head was light and his side was throbbing in heavy, rapid pulsings. He stretched out on his bed and closed his eyes.

23

THE RINGING of the telephone startled him at ten minutes past one. He rolled to his right and picked up the instrument.

"Mr. Gray, a Mr. Sande is in the lobby to see you, sir."

Packard said, "Ask him to give me a minute and then come up."

He hung up and eased himself to his feet, stuffing his tie back into his coat. He took four fresh envelopes out of his suitcase and ripped blank sheets off the writing pad until it was empty. He folded five sheets of the paper together at a time and then folded them double to give bulk and put each of the blank letters into an envelope and sealed it. He slid the telephone book off the shelf of the bed table and dropped it heavily on the desk and sat down and copied four addresses out of the book onto the blank envelopes from different alphabetical sections of the book.

To buy stamps at the desk for one letter made it easy for a clerk to remember an address. If you bought stamps for five it was harder. And if someone stood close to a mailbox and watched you he could spot one white envelope and might get it back from a postman. It would be harder to keep an eye on five; probably impossible to get them back.

He put his report and the four dummies in his inside coat pocket and pulled back the blinds and sat down in the arm-chair with his head back until Sande knocked and he got up with effort to open the door.

"What in the hell are you doin', boy?" was Sande's greeting. "When you're dead, lie down."

He stood in the doorway with an expectant smile and looked around the room. The smile faded.

"Come on in," Packard said.

Packard watched Sande turn his head slightly and look behind the door as he came into the room.

"What's the matter with you?" Packard asked him.

"Me? Why nothin'."

Sande sat down on the edge of the bed. The weight of his body made the soft springs sag badly.

"How did you find me?"

"It wasn't hard. I wrote up a little story on last night, figurin' I was best qualified to speak, and I called the police to see if they'd found out anything new. Which they had."

Packard was pulling the desk chair slowly from the washbasin over to the end of the bed.

"What?"

"Where you lived."

Packard sat down heavily.

"Sarah said you didn't mention the man in the canal."

"Oh, him. I forgot all about him. What do you know?" Sande opened his eyes wide with false surprise.

"I hope he doesn't float."

"Yeah. That's right. I didn't think about that. Here."

Sande twisted some folded yellow sheets from his overcoat pocket and handed them to Packard.

"I was comin' to the l'Europe this mornin' to see how you made out and I thought you might like to keep up on things. My story's there. It's not much. I left out the details. And Tommy Robertson's work on the interview last night. It went out today."

Packard read the blue type. He handed Sande's story back to him without looking up and then glanced at his watch. One-twenty.

"That sounds all right," he said. "Thanks for sparing me."

"Don't mention it. I was sparin' me too."

Packard read through Robertson's story and read it through again and sat holding the yellow pages.

"Did Sarah say that?" he asked Sande.

Sande smiled.

"Well, Tommy thought that's what she meant to say. Or maybe what she ought to say. It's a little strong about how much she's changed her mind, or her not wantin' to go on into Russia. But you might've got that out of what she said. If you tried as hard as Tommy."

His drawl was innocent and pleased at the joke.

"When will it come out?"

"Today over here. This mornin' or tonight at home. It's earlier there. Doornbos had it pretty much the same in *De Telegraaf* this mornin', I hear."

Packard shook his head, wondering to himself if this had put the final pressure on Farrel. It must have contributed.

166

"It might do more harm than good," he said.

"How so?"

"It might make the Russians mad."

"Now that'd be too bad."

Packard handed the pages over.

"It could be," he said. He looked at his watch again.

"Am I keepin' you?"

Packard stood up and rested one hand on the back of the desk chair.

"I have to go back before I'm missed," he said.

"Boy you better go to bed. You're about the color of the sky out there."

"I'll lie down at the L'Europe. Walk over with me and say hello to Sarah."

Sande looked at him.

"Where do you think she is?" he asked.

Packard knew what Sande had been looking for when he walked in now.

"She's at the L'Europe."

Sande shook his head.

"No she isn't, Packard. I know she's not there."

"How do you know? She's in the dining room!"

"No, sir. She's not. When I went into the hotel she was just hurryin' out. I tried to stop her and Farrel and some fellow came along right behind her and the fat boy said to me, 'We have no time for you today, Mr. Sande. Mr. Gray's health is very bad!' "

Sande was imitating Farrel's pompous voice.

"And they went on out the door. I thought of hangin' on to them, but I hurried up to her room to have a look at you, and then I came on over here. Hey! Take it easy, boy!"

Packard was struggling clumsily with his reversible.

"What time was that?"

"About a quarter to one."

Sande stood up and took the coat out of Packard's hands and helped him into it.

"Was the man with Farrel colored?"

"No. A big, heavy-set dish-faced white boy. What are you goin' to do?"

"Have you got a car?"

"The office has one if the girl's not off shoppin' in it."

"Get it, will you? And wait out in front of the L'Europe for me. Don't come in. I'll be out when I can. You won't miss me."

"Where are we goin'?"

"I don't know."

He didn't. You couldn't race through the canals and

streets of Amsterdam shouting out the window. There were things to be done first. Then with luck, you could go somewhere.

"Can you do it?" Packard asked him without looking back. He opened the door.

"Sure. I can. It'll take a while. What's goin' on?"

"I don't know. You might find out if you're around."

Sande said, "You're a mysterious fellow."

Sande pulled the door shut. Packard was already limping along the corridor, leaning forward, trying to hurry. Sande caught up with him and went down the stairs beside him, slowly, ready to help, his heavy hands hanging loosely at his sides. They didn't talk. Packard stopped at the bottom of the stairs and leaned against the bannister, panting.

"You better go easy," Sande said to him.

"I'll go easy. You hurry up."

Sande turned away from him and walked out through the front door. Lunch had been called and the lobby was empty. Packard went across to the desk, taking the letters from his pocket as he went. He took one of the dummies and put it on the counter. The clerk picked it up and held it.

"I'd like stamps for that, please."

The clerk hefted it in his hand, then laid it on a small scale. He opened a drawer and tore off a single stamp and put it on the letter. He dropped it on top of a small pile of other letters and turned back.

"And for these," Packard said. He dropped the four other letters together onto the counter. The clerk looked at them and sharply at Packard.

"Is that all of them?"

"That's all."

The clerk began weighing them one at a time, reading each of them. He held the last one up.

"Ah," he said. "Is it possible? You know Mr. Noyen?"

It was one of the names Packard had copied from the telephone book. God in heaven!

"Only slightly," he said.

"But, if you excuse me, Mr. Gray, this is very surprising."

"Why is it? I'm in some hurry."

"Of course," the clerk said.

And he leaned his elbows on the counter.

"But Mr. Noyen is the cousin of my wife! Where did you meet?"

"Is that so? Well, what a small world. We met in business," Packard said. He took his left hand out of his pocket and checked his watch.

"This is very strange. You know, certainly, that he is ill?"

"Oh? Yes. Of course. That's why I'm writing him. How is he?"

"Worse. Worse," the clerk said and shook his head sadly. "I must tell this to my wife."

"Please do that. Now the stamps?"

"Ah, yes."

The clerk weighed the last letter. He tore the stamps from a blue sheet and began sticking them in place.

"Perhaps I could carry this one for you?"

It was the letter to the cousin of his wife.

"I'll mail it. Thanks anyway."

"But what a surprise."

"Yes. Isn't it?"

The clerk gathered up the letters.

"I'll take those with me, please."

Packard was sweating heavily, leaning hard on the counter.

"But the postman will come directly."

"Give them to me! Will you! Right now! Please!"

"Very well, then. Of course. Here they are, sir."

The clerk's narrow face was drawn in, offended. Packard pushed away from the counter and started for the door unevenly.

"Mr. Gray. The stamps!"

"Add them to my bill," Packard called and he went through the doors and stood at the top of the shallow steps, looking around, with effort and only because he knew he ought to, seeing nothing in the pattern of the street that caught his eye. He turned left, away from the Hotel de l'Europe and walked along the curve of the sidewalk.

The afternoon wind was fresh and cold. The high stones of the buildings looked darker and dirtier against the gray sky and the smell of snow was in the air again. Packard walked as far as the corner, in a straight path, his head down, with the noon crowd dressed in the drab, heavy browns of winter breaking around him, before he found a mailbox fixed to the side of a building, bright red, bulging, grilled. It stuck out from the wall like an old-fashioned stove. Packard, revived by the wind, looked around casually as though unsure of directions.

A man across the street in a brown suitcoat over a black sweater, with baggy brown trousers above black canvas tennis shoes, stopped at the same time, and looked away as Packard continued to stare at him. He hunted in his pockets until he took out a cigarette and tried to light it, turning his head to the gray stone wall against the wind. And Packard took a step and pulled down the chute of the mailbox and

169

dropped his letters in and stepped away. The man was just straightening up.

Packard walked into the street. There were no cars, only bicycles whose riders came close to him deliberately and then turned their heads back after they missed him and shouted. He went across the street and into the Doelen Hotel on the corner. He limped slowly down the four steps inside the lobby and along to the curved desk in the far right corner.

"I want to send a telegram," he told the clerk who came up to him. The man took a pad from below the counter and laid it in front of him.

Packard wrote URGENT I SEE YOU on the form. He addressed it to Mr. I. F. den Hartog at Post Office Box 11732, Main Post Office, Amsterdam. He shoved it toward the clerk.

"When will that go out?"

"I will phone immediately. Ah!" The clerk looked at the form. "You have no other address for it?"

"No."

The clerk was a small round man in a black morning coat and a gray tie. His face was sad and long suffering. He wagged his head.

"I do not know then."

"Suppose you just try it."

"Oh, that I will do. I will call and see and they will tell me how much it will be, too."

"That's the spirit. I also want to use a telephone."

"There is a box over there."

"May I have some change?"

Packard took the money and turned away and walked to the booth, looking carefully back down the long, narrow lobby, and nothing held his attention. He closed the door and leaned against the wooden side, closing his eyes momentarily.

The telegram might be useless, probably was. He did not know when Lois serviced the mailbox, usually twice a day. Early and late. Late was too late.

He leaned up and lifted the receiver and got the operator and leaned back to wait while the Continental telephone service clicked and crackled and jabbered and performed the prescribed mysteries of its delays. And finally there was a response. An American girl answered by repeating the telephone number.

"May I speak with Mr. Mayer. It is urgent."

"Who is calling, please?"

"Packard."

A pause. The booth was hot and close and smelled of old
170

perfume. Packard opened the door and felt the coolness. He closed it when Mayer answered.

"Hello."

"Mr. Mayer?"

"Yes."

"This is Packard."

"Packard. You met a friend of mine recently. Do you remember his name?"

"John. With kitchen matches."

"What can we do for you, Packard?"

Mayer's voice was flat and businesslike over the wires.

"I had something with me here in Amsterdam. I have lost it. Or I think it was stolen. I have to talk to someone about it."

"Was this the package you acquired in Bonn?"

"That's right."

"I'll have someone call you immediately. Where are you?"

"I'll be in the Hotel de l'Europe, room 212, after ten or fifteen minutes."

"Very well. It is fortunate you remembered this number, isn't it?"

Mayer wasn't able to resist it, this chance to remind him of the uncomfortable meeting in Frankfurt where Packard had been so arrogant as to forget the legend that only the European was fit by nature and necessity to be a good clandestine agent. It was a hallowed fact, clung to by a few American Intelligence chiefs faced with a new world history that had them playing in an ancient game seriously for the first time. It was carefully nurtured by those Europeans who had come to assist and advise them and stayed sometimes to think for them. The Old Professionals. Always there, ready to save the Johnny-come-lately's like Packard. The indispensables. It was a bad legend and sometimes it got the wrong policy in the wrong place.

"Sure," Packard said. His voice was tired. "It was just luck that I didn't lose it. Just do what you can, will you?"

"I'll do what is necessary, of course."

Packard hung up and stood bent over the telephone. He straightened up and pushed the door open and went back to the desk. The clerk stared at his face as he approached, then lowered his eyes and picked up a piece of paper.

"It was a great surprise to me," he said. "They sent the telegram."

"This is the weather for surprises, all right. How much?"

He paid and walked out of the lobby. The wind that cleared his head also blew against him in the direction he was going now, holding him back and tiring him. He looked at his wrist watch obviously. One-forty. So late! He was already so late. Then, still holding his arm up, he looked around him in the street as if searching for a clock to compare against his watch.

He lowered his left arm and put it in his pocket and walked on, staring down at the pavement. He had seen the man in the brown suit with his black sweater and black canvas tennis shoes, on the opposite side of the street again, trying to walk in step with two businessmen, on the inside of them, to keep out of sight.

Then this one was no ghost. But he was a flunky, a Party hack, out of place in the office crowd on the streets at noon. They weren't very worried about him to put a tail like that on him. Or they were using their good people for something else.

Packard turned aside to walk around a man standing on the sidewalk slowly grinding out a jangling Paris melody on a painted barrel organ, across the street from the Pays-Bas. Packard reached in his pocket and made a brief mysterious ceremony of putting two coins into the man's hand and shuffled on, smiling to himself. Let the hack work that into his report: Subject made suspicious contact with an organ grinder. Description follows.

He turned in through the lobby door of the Hotel de l'Europe without looking back.

24

AT THE DESK, Packard had to discuss Sarah's key, which they did not want to give him. Miss Borsen had left no instructions about it and it was her room. It was, after all, her room. Beyond doubt. On the other hand, the American Embassy expected him to be there and the doctor and even, yes, the police. Quite so. This had to be admitted. And he did not, indeed, lend favor to the atmosphere of the lobby by waiting there. No, that was certain. Well, then, all right, but it would have to be discussed with Miss Borsen immediately upon her return.

Packard waited in front of the elevator. When it reached the ground floor and the door slid open, the American family filed out. Tacy and her sister first, in identical Tartan skirts and short, red jackets. Packard stepped back to let them go past him. They stopped while the father consulted a schedule.

"Boy!" He heard the older sister's voice as he waited in the elevator. "Did he tie one on!"

"Liddy!" Her mother's whisper was harsh.

Tacy looked back at him in the elevator and he winked at her as she stared.

"He's hurt," she said to her father, worried.

"Man, he sure is." The father laughed loudly without looking up from the schedule, and even the mother smiled. Packard leaned back against the wall of the elevator where he could not see them.

Down the corridor and around the two corners, the telephone began ringing as Packard turned the key in Sarah's door. With the talk at the desk and his wound it had taken fifteen minutes to get this far from the Doelen. You might operate around Generals and Presidents. Corporals, clerks, and assistants could ruin you. Would ruin you.

The telephone was ringing and he closed the door with the key hanging in the lock behind him and went along Sarah's little hallway, across the empty, deserted room, between the beds, and answered it. A man was at the other end.

"Packard?"

"Yes."

"My name is David. I just had a call from the south that you wanted to talk to me. Give me your passport number, will you?"

Packard sat down on the edge of Sarah's bed and took the green book from his inside pocket and read the number out of the narrow window in the front of the cover. There was a pause.

"All right. There is a girl in Amsterdam that you have wanted to meet. What is the first letter of her name?"

"L."

"Swell. I'm calling for Lois, Packard."

The recognition was complete.

"We've heard about your accident. How are you?"

"Pretty shaky."

"Need anything? Medically? Did you get our present?"

"I do when there's time, and I got the cigars, thanks. I called you because the girl is gone. Do you know Farrel?"

"We've heard of him."

"She left with him and another man at twelve forty-five. I was to meet her here at one. She promised to stay in the hotel. Unless she changed her mind, she wouldn't have gone willingly. I don't believe she did."

"Who was the other man?"

"A friend told me. I didn't see them. No one I've met, unless I met him in Brussels."

"A friend you say?"

David's voice was calm, almost placid—Packard imagined him leaning back in his swivel chair with his feet on

173

the desk—but it was alert. Its business was dealing with excited agents, all of them announcing that the world had only five minutes more. All demanding immediate action. Packard had been on that end of the phone, too. He tried to keep it in mind. David was leaning back and thinking and trying to put the pieces together calmly with what could be asked and told over the telephone.

"A newspaperman," Packard answered his question. "He was with me last night. I think he's all right. Bob Sande. S-A-N-D-E. *Herald Tribune.*"

"Did she take her luggage?"

Packard looked around the shadowy room, gray in the light of the winter's afternoon, at the bottles on the dressing table, the suitcase open on the stand. He looked into the corner between the green couch and the window.

"Not all of it. I don't see her typewriter and briefcase."

"So she went in a hurry. Or she isn't going far."

"She went in a hurry. And they want something from her. Like a letter on her own typewriter."

"They don't have the letter yet?"

"They didn't two hours ago."

"Well, thank God for small favors, anyway."

David's voice was relieved, less concerned after he heard it.

Packard got impatient. Suddenly. There had been too many clerks, too much Dickson, too much pain. It was getting too late. He picked a yellow capsule and two codeine tablets out of the piles that Sarah had built inside the lamp on the bedside table and made saliva in his mouth and gulped them through his throat.

"Will the Dutch co-operate? Can you get them to screen off the border roads and airports?" he demanded.

"And boats?" he added.

"If we have enough reason."

"Well what the hell is this, then?"

David's laugh was appeasing. "Take it easy," he said.

"It's five after two," Packard said flatly. "She's been gone an hour and a quarter. You can walk out of this country in two hours."

"That gives us forty-five minutes," David said gently. "Can you tell me why you think she went unwillingly?"

"I think I'd gotten that far. We were in good shape until our employer's man Friday came in here this morning and blew me wide open. But Farrel got himself in trouble, too. So I don't think she was ready to go anywhere. With anybody."

There was a long pause. Packard could hear the scratch and whistle of breath. David was lighting a cigarette.

174

"I haven't heard about this morning."

"He might not be anxious to tell it. I wrote you a letter about it. I also sent a telegram. You can skip the telegram now. How about it?"

Packard needed the help and the support. But the weakness was growing in him. The telephone was heavy and slippery in the cold sweat of his palm. His forehead and body were wet too and he sat on the bed, leaning his body forward on his knees, bent almost double to ease the throbbing. He knew he had to want to go on. And he had to want Sarah safe and alive. But what he felt above it all was a numb hypnotizing weariness so that he had to keep remembering the urgencies mechanically. So much talk. Get it over. Do something or don't do something. But get it over. Get it over.

"The object of this exercise—" David began.

And Packard knew he wouldn't get the help he wanted and he started to hang up but it called for less effort to sit there slumped over, listening.

"—was for you to do the thing as an individual. If I call on the Dutch to stop her and we find out she is going somewhere legally and voluntarily, we've done just what the boss said not to do. We've blocked her with force and in the name of the Great White Father. Are you still with me?"

"I'm here," Packard said, resigned. "We can lose both ways, but my way we might win; or we might get the girl back anyway."

David's voice lost none of its patience.

"You might be wrong, Packard. She might not want to be back."

He might be wrong. He had made a mistake with John and John was dead in Brussels. He had the weighted, futile sensation of swimming in clear glue with heavy, dripping arms. You didn't get anywhere. And you wore yourself down and you finally sank. But if you quit you sank, too, without trying. He felt his halfheartedness too and was angry with it. Halfheartedly.

"I might be, but I'm not. I'm handling this. She wouldn't leave willingly!"

"After this morning?"

"She didn't take her luggage."

"Then she'll probably be back. And they don't have the letter, which is the big half of it if the analysis you made for our friend is right."

"Hell yes, that's the big thing. All they have is the girl. And we've got lots of girls. I'm on a job. I've told you the kind of help I need. I'd like to get it!"

175

David said firmly, "This is my area. I can't do what you want."

Packard was tired. He could see the other man's point too well. Sarah was part of an assignment, to David, covered by orders. Worth certain risks; not worth others.

"Okay," he said. "Sorry I bothered you. Don't stick your neck out."

The lost argument and his inability to bring himself out of a depressed uncertainty were making him petulant and peevish; childish. And he knew it and it made him worse.

"You're like State. Lots of results but no risks."

"Easy," David said sternly. "This is a public wire."

"And it's a public two-fifteen. She's ten miles farther away."

"All right," David said. "Listen. You knew there was someone else on this with you?"

"I heard it. But I haven't seen anyone else in a bandage."

David laughed, trying to snap him out of it.

"You're just lucky."

"You stay there," he went on, "and take it easy. If the girl's with Farrel, Farrel is covered and I'll hear something. As soon as I do, I'll call you. How's that?"

"It's something. I told you what we ought to do."

"If we get any proof you're right we'll do it, too."

"That's fine. Get Moscow to confirm it. Where can I call you?"

David was silent over the wire. He didn't want to give out the number, but he didn't want to refuse Packard again. Finally he gave a number.

"Thanks," Packard said ironically. "I'll call you if she walks in."

"Do that. In the meantime sit tight until I call."

Packard forced himself. "Why don't you ask the Dutch to watch for her without picking her up? At least we'll know which way she went. Or how."

"Let's wait and hear on Farrel."

"Nobody on their side is waiting. Sarah isn't waiting."

Packard heard words coming from the instrument as he raised it slowly with his right hand. The mouthpiece bumped on the glass top of the table and he fumbled it against the cradle before he finally got it hung up.

He raised his head and looked slowly around the room again. A faint scent of Sarah's perfume hung in the air of it. He looked at the spot on the couch where she had smiled up at him over the top of her newspaper. He turned his eyes and stared at the door trying to bring back the image of her as she stood there in her red skirt and black sweater, fingering the gold medallion, her thin face worried, wanting to believe him, wanting to love him, afraid of her doubts. But all that came to him strongly from this deliberate effort at self-torment, all that he could feel was the dying emptiness in the room and the loneliness that she had left him. His throat and face muscles tightened and his eyes burned.

He straightened up in reaction to the emotion and reached across with his right hand and pulled the telephone off its cradle and waited for the desk to answer. He looked at his watch. Two twenty-five.

David was wrong. David had orders and Packard had no proof, but he was wrong and Packard could understand him but he could not wait while he was wrong.

"Get me the police," he said to the operator. "Never mind what the matter is. Just please let me talk with the police."

He felt stronger with the action and he understood the reason for his uncertainty with David, and his giving way to physical weariness. As long as he believed she might have left because she wanted to, he could not justify a fight. But he looked around the gray, empty room with her perfume still soft in the air and remembered her and his doubt was gone.

"Is there someone who speaks English?" he said into the phone. "Good. I hope you can help me. I am an American. Packard Gray. I'm in the hotel room of my fiancée, Sarah Borsen, which is room 212 at the Hotel de l'Europe."

He gave them his right name. After last night they had it on file anyway.

"I was to meet Miss Borsen at twelve-thirty here. She has never arrived, but some of her baggage is missing. A man named Farrel . . ."

He repeated the name.

". . . lives in this hotel, too. He followed her out of the hotel at a quarter to one."

Touch it up some. Not too much.

"A friend of mine, a newspaper reporter, saw them and told me. No. It's not possible that she would stay away so long without calling me. In many years she has never done that. It isn't like her. I know that Farrel has bothered her before and she was afraid of him. I have also looked and find that her passport is gone. He may try to take her out of the country."

The passport must be gone. Her purse was gone. That's where she carried it. In a leather folder.

"I know this sounds extreme, but I am frightened for her. I know how she felt about this man. And it will not look good for you either if an American girl disappears in this way."

177

That might help or it might only annoy them. It was probably his strongest argument.

"She is an American. I don't know what he is. Yes, I'll notify the Embassy, but can't you do something now? At the borders? Or the airports? No, I don't have a picture, but the newspapers will. She is very well known."

He gave careful descriptions of Farrel and Sarah.

"Thank you," he said finally. "Thank you very much. I know you will. But hurry. Of course I'll call if she returns."

He slid the receiver back into place. He swung his legs onto Sarah's bed and bunched the pillow under its red spread beneath his head. And in the darkening room, with his overcoat still on, he closed his eyes.

Well, it was done. Let it come now. If he was wrong, too bad. They could chew on him in Washington. But it was his assignment. As long as it was, he would handle it. Just like this. Without David and his orders or his help if that was the way he had to do it. A man had a right to worry about the girl he might marry, officially or unofficially.

His stretched-out body began to relax with the codeine.

Probably would marry.

He grinned through his drowsiness. It was a pleased grin. Certainly ought to marry.

"Damn it," he said aloud. "This is no time for sleep!"

He opened his eyes, but with the drugs the pain was softening in his side and chest. He began to breathe freely and fully as it eased, and in the freedom from pain and the warmth of the room, relief and drowsiness, again, held him. Could he be doing something else? No.

"Five minutes," he said aloud.

He looked at his watch. Two thirty-five. He set the hands at two forty-five in his mind and closed his eyes.

Ten minutes. I need it. The machine is fatigued. Just ten minutes.

25

PACKARD opened his eyes. He opened them and stared up at the ceiling, dusky in the late, dark light, and thought that the telephone bell must have been a part of his dream. Then the fact of the darkness disturbed him vaguely through senses numbed by fatigue and the drug, and he pulled his left arm up to look at his watch. At the same time, he heard a soft voice beside him and jerked his head to the left.

178

He moved his eyes up the form standing there and had an instant when his heart skipped and pounded, startled and alarmed at the helplessness of being caught this way, so that he wanted to close his eyes and hide again in sleep.

The big Negro standing over him, talking into the telephone softly, had heard his movement and turned his head and looked down at him, and in the twilight darkness, Packard could see the cloudy whites of his eyes staring flatly at him out of the black face.

"Sure. I'll give him the message," were the first words Funston said to the phone that Packard understood.

These were the bad seconds, when you were surprised, the ones between when you found you needed courage and before it came to you. They weren't many, but long and bad.

"Give me that telephone!" Packard said loudly with a remote knowledge that the person on the other end of the wire should hear him and be warned. The few words broke the spell of shock and brought some physical control of his body. His mind still lumbered haltingly.

The Negro shook his head slightly and continued to listen. Packard lifted his legs off the right side of the bed, away from the telephone, conscious of his pain only as a distant beginning. He unbuttoned the bottom button of his overcoat, sitting. Then he stood up and started carefully around the end of the bed.

"Give me that telephone," he ordered again. His voice was thick.

"Nothin'," Funston told the telephone. "It's all right. No, I better give him the message. He doesn't look wide awake. You just go ahead and tell it to me."

The Negro revolved slowly to face Packard, shifting the receiver to his left hand, so big that it covered most of the instrument. He lifted his right hand with the pink palm outward and moved it back and forth, telling Packard to be quiet and wait a minute.

Packard said, "What are you pulling? Give it over, Funston!"

The Negro paid no attention to him. He stood listening. Packard stepped between the two beds and stopped. He measured the size of the Negro and considered his own strength and his wound. Funston pulled his right hand back and held it spread loosely in front of his chest, looking somewhere past Packard, concentrating on the telephone.

"There isn't much he can do about it if he doesn't like it," he said into the mouthpiece.

Packard let his knees sag forward and brought his weight to the balls of his feet. He reached suddenly with his right hand pushing it into his suitcoat pocket for the gun, his eyes

179

fixed on Funston's middle. And his reaching fingers came clumsily onto the big butt of the gun and the trigger guard, because it had rolled upside down in his pocket as he slept. He began the motion to pull it out this way. Then he saw, and opened his hand, and withdrew it slowly from his pocket and let it fall to his side.

The Negro had moved only his hand and wrist. Into his coat and out. He was still giving his attention to the telephone and holding the automatic almost as an afterthought, on a level with Packard's chest.

"You son of a bitch, Funston!" Packard said bitterly.

"He's quiet again now," the Negro said. "No, he doesn't."

He listened. Packard turned and sat down slowly on the bed aware of his danger, but unable to isolate the nature of it. And the throbbing pain began and slowed his thinking. He put his hands on his knees, spread open. The Negro lowered the gun and let it hang straight at his side while Packard watched it carefully, less than three feet away.

"He might," Funston said, now in a natural deep voice, glancing at Packard's face.

Packard saw the unnatural white of his teeth as he smiled. The dull white of his eyes and the bright white of his big teeth and the rest of his features nearly invisible in the gloom. Packard looked down at his watch and read it this time. Four-ten. He had been out for an hour and a half.

"Oh I'll be sure to tell him all right," the Negro said.

Then he said goodbye and felt behind him with the telephone until he hung it up, without turning his head from Packard. He reached with the same hand and switched on the bed light. Packard instinctively ducked his head to keep the sudden glare from slowing his vision. His body was obeying. His mind still struggled and failed to focus.

Funston lifted the gun and looked down at it and smiled again. He put it back under his shoulder with an easy push of his wrist.

"I don't think we'll need this," he said. His teeth stood out whiter yet in the light.

No, he wouldn't need it. He was big enough without it. Why make noise?

Packard got to his feet, knowing he could not get to his gun in time with this man.

"Where is Sarah?" he said.

"I just heard that she is in Copenhagen. I'll tell you about it, Mr. Gray."

"With Farrel?"

"No. Mr. Farrel says that he is on the way back to the hotel here. I want to tell you some things."

He had been talking to Farrel, then, and they had her out.

180

Amsterdam to Copenhagen. Legal travel. Copenhagen to Prague or East Berlin or Warsaw. No problem. But if she was still in Copenhagen.

He swung with his right hand at the Negro. He swung with the joints of his fingers folded over in a sharp wedge, below the chin, into the thick throat. Funston let out a whistling gasp and reached both hands up to his throat, choking, and sat backward onto Packard's bed.

Packard checked his weight, reaching for his gun with his right hand. He felt the pain then, hot and sickening, filling his chest and stomach, as he flopped the gun upright in his hand and pulled back the hammer. He backed away from the beds, panting, pushing his left hand against his side.

"Now! Get away from the telephone!" he said to Funston.

The Negro still sat, his eyes watering, sucking noisily for breath, rubbing his throat with his hands. He shook his head, and tried to speak. Packard stepped forward. The Negro took his right hand from his throat and began to lower it.

"Don't do it! Move out of there or I'll use this. I don't have time for you!"

Funston pointed at the handkerchief in his breast pocket. He pulled it out gingerly in two fingers and wiped his eyes on it and blew his nose. He held it in his hand and said something, urgently, in a cracked, coarse whisper.

Packard leaned forward impatiently to hear, but carefully. The Negro took a deep breath and held it.

"Lois," he said, forcing it out in a long sound.

"What?"

Funston nodded. He pointed a finger at himself.

"Lois," he said again.

He was beginning to be able to get air again. The beads of wetness on his cheeks and forehead glittered in the light from the table. He shook his head and stood up, stuffing the handkerchief into his breast pocket.

"Man," he gasped. "I owe you for that!"

He looked with menace at Packard. Then he grinned and shrugged his shoulders.

"That's no way to treat a lady," he said hoarsely.

Packard held the gun on him, but lower.

"What the hell is this now? Who are you?"

"I'm Jefferson Alois Funston, Mr. Gray. Lois."

Packard thought, his mind finally able to deal with it.

"Who were you talking to?"

"David."

"So? And what's the name of the man you work for?"

"Nick."

"Does he have a business telephone?"

"His home number is zero zero seven zero."

Packard shook his head. He let the hammer forward on the revolver and dropped the gun into his overcoat pocket.

"Glad to meet you," he said without enthusiasm. "Sorry about your throat."

"I started to tell you." The Negro still spoke with effort. "But I didn't think we ought to talk about it while I had the phone off the hook. And I didn't know how far you'd go when you got that gun out, either."

Funston stepped aside to make room for him and Packard sat down on the bed.

"I've never liked the idea of an assistant I had to guess at," he said. "It doesn't help me and someone can get hurt."

The Negro's teeth flashed.

"I find that's true," he said. "Though I'm not exactly an assistant. I'm on Farrel who's a separate problem that begins at home and is run from home. As long as you didn't need to know me, it was better you didn't."

"You could say I needed to know," Packard told him sourly. "If you're on him, what happened. Is Sarah in Copenhagen?"

Funston dropped into the armchair at the end of Packard's bed and looked at his hands.

"I don't know," he said. "I can't tell you that. They went out of the hotel about a quarter to one; Farrel and the girl and another fellow, and I followed them in a cab as far as the docks, beyond the main station. I lost them there."

He looked up at Packard.

"I'm sorry for it," he said, "but my job is Farrel. And I have to keep him trusting me. When they turned down a bare street along the harbor, I couldn't come any closer without him spotting me. So I told the driver to wait. Farrel turned left around a corner at the end of the street and I never picked them up again. You know how hard it is for one man to do a proper surveillance."

"And you're not inconspicuous," Packard said to him, sore because he had let Sarah get away.

"That's right," the Negro answered calmly. "I'm not. But I had you fooled. And I've got a big natural advantage at night."

Packard put his head back and laughed once.

"Okay, Jefferson, you win. What did our boy David have to say?"

The Negro cleared his throat with a rasping effort. He cleared it again, his eyes watering.

"He wanted you to know the Ambassador ate him out good this afternoon on account of you."

182

"Tough," Packard said.

"It appears Farrel showed up at the Embassy playing the important American businessman about three-fifteen and told the Ambassador he was at Schiphol airport putting Miss B on a plane for Copenhagen when the Dutch police stopped them for questioning. According to Farrel she told the police they should mind their own business and so should you. She had a passport, and she wasn't any property of yours, and she knew what she was doing."

The phrase, "She wasn't any property of yours," made a tight feeling of hurt in Packard's chest and then made him angry.

"Farrel wanted an apology for having the police put on him and said he was going to report the whole thing in Washington. So the Ambassador called David and said you caused him great embarrassment and said you were to behave yourself." Funston looked up, out of the tops of his eyes. "You did call the cops, didn't you?"

"Yeah, I called them."

"How come you did that?"

"David wanted to sit tight on his soft side. I thought somebody had better do something to help her.

"I guess she didn't need help," he added bitterly. "Or she didn't want it."

"Maybe. But you'll be interested in the rest of it. David is pretty thorough anyway. He'd already called Copenhagen before he phoned here. KLM had a direct flight there this afternoon at two-thirty. Her name wasn't on the passenger list and Customs had no record of her coming through at that end."

Packard began to watch Funston intently again as he talked.

"And LOT, the Polish airline, flies Mondays, Tuesdays and Thursdays from Copenhagen direct to Warsaw at five-five. It was gone before Copenhagen could get it checked. Today is Thursday, but the flight went out early."

Packard looked at his watch.

"It's only four twenty-five now," he said.

"Five-five there is four-five here. We're an hour earlier. There were five people on the LOT passenger list. Her name wasn't on it. They could only have smuggled her on with fake papers brought out from inside. They could have, if she was willing to go, that is. You can't carry someone kicking and screaming around an airport."

"She said she was."

"Farrel said she was. You saw her after lunch. What did she look like?"

Packard said, "I didn't see her after lunch. I wasn't here."

Funston looked surprised. He edged his chair around and pulled it closer.

"Look here, Packard," he said. "I wouldn't be in such a hurry to disbelieve the girl and take Farrel's word for gospel. That's the trouble in getting to care for someone. You think the worse of them if you believe they've gone against you."

Packard smiled briefly.

"That's one of the troubles," he said.

"They've been watching Farrel for a long time at home," Funston told him. "He's not such a fine fellow. And I've been in the room next to his since Tuesday with a headset and transistor pickup. Even though I can't hear everything, I can make out Farrel was only supposed to help Miss Borsen to go back to Russia and encourage her by telling her she was doing right. And also paying her bills. But he got some big idea of his own, about using this letter of hers, that was going to win the cold war for Russia and make a Deputy Premier out of him. You know what I'm talking about?"

"I might," Packard said. "Get on with it, Jefferson."

The Negro waited until he saw that Packard wasn't going to tell him about it. He sat back in his chair.

"The Party boys visited him around dawn Wednesday morning and they were with him again last night about midnight," he said. "They let him use some of their people in Brussels for something and it appears he turned all hell loose there to no purpose."

"Did you ever know Frank Anderson?" Packard asked him.

"No."

"I'll tell you about him sometime. This was the dawn visit Wednesday?" he prompted.

"That's right. Then last night he went out on his own and tried to get rid of you. About midnight two of them came in and racked him back for it. Really put it on him. They said he'd broken Party discipline, jeopardized Party organization, put his own interests in place of the Party's, and generally had been doing too much of his own thinking for a long spell. They told him that final arrangements were laid on for today and he would either produce the lady without further fuss or he would drop it and expect Party discipline. Mr. Farrel was a very frightened fellow by the time they left. And there wasn't ever a time for me to tell you about it. And I never guessed that producing her meant he'd run off with her."

Packard started to say something, but Funston held up a hand and stopped him and went on.

"I was also in the dining room with him this noon," he

said, "when she came down from you and sat over next to a window, by herself. The waiter brought Farrel a note about twelve-thirty and he got up and went out into the lobby. When he came back he sat down over with her and talked to her, until she jumped up, excited, and left with him. I picked them up when they came back through the lobby. She was carrying a typewriter and a briefcase and had on a trench coat, and she was still excited about something. Excited or stirred up. Another fellow joined them and they all went out together."

He leaned toward Packard.

"And now you know everything I know, what do you think?" he asked.

Packard shifted on the bed to favor the pain in his left side, resenting the need to interrupt his thoughts with movement.

He said, "Jeff, what did Farrel think after the Dickson thing this morning? Did he think he'd won?"

"He thought everybody'd lost; especially him."

Packard nodded in agreement.

"I can tell you what was in the note he got at lunch," he said.

"I can tell it myself, now I know you weren't in the room. That's what I tell you, man. That's why I said I wouldn't be in such a hurry to pass a judgment . . ."

Packard interrupted.

"The note said I'd gone out of her room and left the hotel. That fat, fastidious bastard!"

"Sure. And then all Farrel had to do was tell her he, or somebody, had you off someplace and she'd better do right if she wanted to help you. Were you far enough along with her that she'd go if that happened?"

"I asked her to marry me," Packard said, watching the Negro to see his reaction.

"My, my," Funston grinned and shook his head. "Did you mean it?"

"When I did it, I had to do it. But I mean it."

Packard pushed carefully to his feet. He glanced at the codeine tablets and decided against them and he walked slowly out beyond the ring of light and stood in front of the dressing table, looking down. He reached out and picked up Sarah's perfume bottle and moved it under his nose absently and caught sight of Funston watching him, waiting out the silence of his thinking.

Packard moved over and stood and looked out through the windows at the blank silhouette of the tower in the square across the canal. Snow in large flakes fell steadily between the early evening lights and Sarah's window into the blank water and onto the reflection of yellow lights from the hotel dining room below the traffic on the bridge, and he stood turning the flat oblong shape of the bottle over and over between the fingers of his right hand.

To begin with Farrel. He hadn't gone to the Embassy because of injured dignity. He had other things to worry about. And he hadn't gone to tell them where Sarah was.

"Farrel," Packard said aloud against the window glass, "went to the Embassy to get them to call off the cops."

"I said that," Funston answered him softly.

Packard was impatient, with the excitement of hope beginning.

"But he wanted them called off before they had a chance to stop her at a border or ask her any questions," he said. "That's the point."

Funston said nothing. Packard turned abruptly and sat down on the arm of the green couch.

"The police never did stop them at the airport," he said; "or ask them any questions. I'll bet they never went to an airport." He looked up. "You tell me Farrel got to the Embassy at three-fifteen?"

"That's what David said."

"Jeff, you've been on him. You know about him. Where would Farrel go? Where would you look for him right now?"

"He told the Ambassador he was coming back here to pack."

"You know that's crap, Jeff. Just like the airport is crap. Don't use up our time. Farrel knows damned well what I am, and he knows I'll hear whatever he told the Ambassador. So she isn't in Copenhagen and he won't be here. Where would you look for him?"

"Well, that depends."

"We're in a hurry," Packard said.

"Well, that depends," Jeff said stubbornly, "on whether he got her safely out on schedule or not."

"What if he did?"

"Then he'd believe he doesn't have to worry except for you. And you can't prove anything. He doesn't know about me, and he doesn't know they've been watching him at home. Anyway we think he doesn't. So I suppose he'd just go on as he has been, and we can wait here for him."

"But since he isn't coming here, because he told the Ambassador he would, he hasn't got her out, if you're right. Not yet anyway. What then?"

"Why, then the Party's after him. You're after him. And if she's alive anywhere he's got to count on her telling about

186

him, so he's finished at home too. I'd guess him to go somewhere to make it hard for the Party to assassinate him and somewhere hard to extradite him from. With that kind of a choice I'd go to Switzerland. Good police, a small country hard to get away with anything in, jealous of neutrality."

Packard stood up. He began to button his reversible and the Negro got to his feet, watching him.

"What would you do if you weren't sure whether she was out or not?" Packard asked.

"When I think about it, I'd go to Switzerland no matter what happened. Even if he gets her out, they've got too much against him. All that breaking Party discipline, and that stuff. If he's smart he'll figure he's got a poor future. And I guess he's that smart."

"So do I. And I'd hurry if I figured that way. Let's get to the airport, Jeff, and find out if we're good enough to be in this business."

Jeff came past the edge of the light, into the shadows, and stood beside Packard.

Packard said, "You give me three or four minutes, then come down. We shouldn't be seen together. You're still clean and there was a man on me when I came in at two. A paunchy little hack in a brown suit and a black sweater and black tennis shoes. When you come down, go out of the hotel and turn left; across the bridge toward the tower and the square. Get on the right-hand side and wait at the far side of the bridge. I'll pick you up. If Sande is down there, we'll go with him. If he isn't, I'll have a cab. Either way, I'll be in the back seat with my face where you can see it. Okay?"

He started toward the entrance hallway.

"Wait a minute, Packard."

He stopped and turned.

"What do we do with Farrel if we get him? I'm not finished with him. We want to know his friends for our people here. And we want more on his publishing house. That's why we haven't blown the whistle on him yet. And a lot of work's gone into getting me this close. You keep that in mind."

"What I'll keep in mind," Packard answered passionately, "is that Farrel had his goons beat one of us to death in Brussels Tuesday night. And I'll keep in mind that he knows where Sarah is and I think she's still around, and if I find him he's going to tell me where she is. You believe that. He'll have her ripped in two to get that letter out of her while she's still in a Western country. Only a big, flashy, successful coup will save him now with the Party. And they'll kill her if they get the letter. Job or no job, that son of a bitch is finished if I catch him. Now let's not get in each other's way, Jeff."

He turned along the hallway without waiting for an answer. He waited impatiently while Funston swung the door shut behind them and pulled out the key that Packard had left hanging and dropped it in his pocket.

"I'll just walk along the hall with you," the Negro said. "When we get near the elevator I'll wait."

They walked the empty corridor rapidly in spite of Packard's wound and the twist it gave his body as he bent into it. They went without words until they turned the corner that led to the elevator, and Funston stopped.

"I'll stand here and give you time," he said. "What is it makes you think she's still around?"

Packard looked up, ready to tell him "later" again, until he saw Funston's expression.

This would be a bad time to lose the Negro. And if he didn't justify how he thought and what he had in mind for Farrel if he caught him, he was going to lose him. Not only lose him but have him against him. Maybe calling David to have him stopped. Maybe doing it himself. Farrel still was Funston's pigeon.

"All right," he said. "I think so because Farrel didn't know whether she got out or not. He wasn't with her. He was at the Embassy at three-fifteen anyway. That means she was still inside Holland then and he thought there was time to get the cops off before she reached a border; or he wouldn't have bothered. It takes a while to change an order, too. You said the Copenhagen plane went at two-thirty. I didn't call the cops until two-thirty, so they never stopped him at Schiphol. Some loyal Dutch police official reported to the Party that I had called the cops, and the Party got it to Farrel and he ran to the Ambassador with his story."

"The Embassy didn't know anything about Farrel, did it?" he asked.

"Naturally not."

"We always keep the wrong secrets from each other. Anyway, Farrel is going somewhere until he knows which way the fallout is drifting. And where you say is as good as any place. It's worth a try, isn't it?"

"It sounds like you thought it all through."

"Okay then. Let's move out. If you're with me?"

The Negro had the fingertips of both hands resting lightly on his hips.

"I'm coming, all right," he said, "just to protect my investment if you find him. I'd like Mr. Farrel alive. So

188

would Nick. If Sande is down there, remember you and I are only acquaintances."

"I'll have that in mind, too," Packard said.

He walked along to the elevator. He looked at the indicator arrow and pushed the button. He reached for Sarah's perfume bottle and rolled it in his hand while he waited, and it rattled against the gun in his overcoat pocket until he took it out and moved it to the other pocket.

26

PACKARD opened the back door of Sande's gray Ford sedan and got in and pulled the door shut. He leaned against the cushions with the relief that sitting down brought to his chest. Sande turned around from the driver's seat.

"Hey," he said. "Come on up front and be sociable. What about Sarah?"

"I don't know. We're down to playing hunches."

He changed the subject.

"It's a little more comfortable back here where I can stretch. Did you wait here long?"

"Twenty or thirty minutes. I called to say I'd be late and Sarah's room didn't answer. So I took a chance on waiting for you to come back in. I couldn't leave the car in this traffic anyway. It took me so long because our girl went home in the car to get dressed so she could leave the office early for a date tonight."

Packard smiled.

"You pay her for that?"

"Overtime. Plus travel mileage. Where are we goin'?"

Packard raised his head to look across the street at the hotel entrance. Traffic was heavy in the dark evening street. Bicycle riders had their lamps on and their heads down against the big snowflakes that fell thickly, straight down, and melted wetly against their clothing and on the shining streets. The horns of cars piling up on the bridge were dulled by the insulation of snow and the light from the high lamps on the bridge were blurred yellow. In the crowded streets he couldn't tell whether he was being watched or not. He didn't care.

"To the airport at Schiphol. In a minute," he said. "I told a fellow we'd give him a ride out there."

He watched people go in through the hotel doors and stamp their feet and brush their hands across the shoulders of their coats. Half a dozen got as far as the door from the

inside and saw that it was snowing and went back to the
desk to call a cab or go up to their rooms again for more
clothes. Time was pushing hard against him inside, but when
he saw Funston swing through the doors and come out into
the street he looked at his watch. It had taken him only four
minutes.

Funston paused on the sidewalk, letting the flow of people
break by him, and looked around casually. Then he turned
easily and started for the bridge. Packard watched him
walking tall and broad above the crowd, his head high,
ignoring the snow, until he crossed the street and was out
on the center of the bridge.

"Okay," Packard said. "I see him. Let's go. Across the
bridge there."

Sande looked back at him curiously as he started the
motor.

"Which one is he?"

"It's all right. I have him in sight. Just pull ahead."

Sande pulled out from the curb and eased steadily into
the flow of traffic, disrupting it, getting yelled at.

"If we wait for them to stop for us," he explained, "we'll
get ourselves snowed in for the winter."

Packard looked through the back window. There were
too many lights behind him, too much movement. He could
tell nothing from the pattern. He put his face against the
side window as they crossed the bridge. Funston had stopped
at the far corner and stood loosely, his hands in his pockets,
watching the traffic and waiting.

"There he is," Packard said. "The big Negro. Stop right
there at the end."

Sande glanced back again.

"Is that Funston? Farrel's writer boy?"

"Yeah."

"You're movin' in strange circles," Sande said as he pulled
the car against the curb and stopped. A policeman in white
gloves and a white cape in the street began to blow his
whistle in blasts and waved at them with short angry jerks
of his arm as traffic piled up behind them. Jeff looked down
at the window and saw Packard. He pulled open the front
door and rolled his body into the car and shut the door,
again in one sudden trick athletic movement. Sande let the
car go forward.

"Bob, this is Jeff Funston," Packard said. "Jeff, Bob
Sande."

"Hi," Sande said, concentrating on the traffic. "I've heard
of you. That's the Munt Plein," he said to Packard over his
shoulder.

He waved his hand as they turned diagonally across a

190

square, bright under neon lights, looking like Christmas with the snow, the dark tower that Packard had seen from Sarah's room to the left. Streetcars were stopped across the square, their doors choked with crowds jamming to get aboard.

"Mr. Farrel mentioned you to me, too," the Negro said. "Is it all right if I ride in the front with you, Mr. Sande?"

In his cover again, Funston had gone back to the soft-voiced, carefully precise diction and sarcasm.

"You're the boy with the prejudices, accordin' to your good friend Farrel. Suit yourself. I'm a literary fellow. We don't have prejudices."

"I'm encouraged to hear that," Jeff said. "What do you write?"

They bore right, down a street where the shop windows blazed against the snow and the traffic on the narrow sidewalks spilled over into the streets in the evening rush. Packard watched the snow fall against the lights and then into the bare trees of a square that they came to, surrounded by cabarets and cafés, and onto the black glistening waters of a canal beyond the square. He closed his eyes and stretched his legs to the left in the back seat and thought of what they could have done with Sarah and the layout of Schiphol airport as he remembered it from the day before, and where to look for Farrel there. Funston and Sande were still going at each other in the front seat and he did not listen. There was nothing more he could do in the car. He opened his eyes once, when the whining wheels rutted into streetcar rails and the car skidded shortly on the dark, slick cobblestones. He saw the black hollowness of a park to his left, down the sidestreets, between regular squat rows of red brick houses. Then he closed them again and dozed off uneasily.

Packard sat up quickly when the car stopped. Beyond his window rose the mass of the new airport buildings, looking white under the hard glare of many lights. Floodlights lit up the entrance and the walls and the glass of the large window. On top, above the railings of the observation platform, red and green warning lights glowed. Snowflakes floated clear and individually in the swinging blue-white beam of the field beacon. Packard heard and felt the shaking roar of a big plane taking off under full power and the harsh crackle of a public address system calling out flights inside the building. Sande turned around and draped his right arm across the back of the front seat.

"You get out here," he said. "I'll park this."

Packard looked at his watch. Five-five.

Funston opened the door and stepped out.

191

"Thank you very much, Mr. Sande," he said. "I hope I was no trouble for you."

"Sure," Sande said. "Anytime."

The Negro leaned down through the open door.

"Thank you, Mr. Gray. I'll run along now."

"So long," Packard said offhandedly.

Funston straightened up and closed the door carefully. He turned and walked in through the entrance doors, shaking his head at a porter who spoke to him.

Packard opened the door.

"I'm looking for Farrel," he said to Sande. "If I find him I might need all the help I can get. If you spot him, grab him and yell out."

He paused.

"You don't have to. There could be some guns."

"You got one?"

"I've got one."

"How about him bein' around here?"

Sande pointed after Funston with a gesture of his thick hand.

"Don't worry about him. Just find Farrel. I'll see you inside. Thanks for the ride."

"I'll be right along. I don't mind grabbin' Mr. Farrel. Try not to hit me fatally in my writin' hand."

Packard stepped out and slammed the door shut. He took a deep breath of the cold wet air and looked around, and spotted nothing to bother him. He walked in through the doors. Funston was just inside.

"Call David," Packard said to him. "Tell him where we are and tell him to get the police back on the borders if he can. Tell him why. Then check the ticket and information places and see when something goes to Switzerland or Frankfurt. If we get lost I'll meet you here. If you find him, get him to me."

"Why yes sir."

"For Christ's sake, Jeff, don't be like that. This is my last chance."

It was in Packard's voice. How much the girl meant to him. Not the assignment now. Not a cause. Not even Farrel. Just Sarah. One loved human being. The Negro heard it and understood him.

"Okay then," he said. "Let's get to it."

Packard looked back over his shoulder.

"There comes Sande," he said. They both moved off alone.

There was movement and noise inside the building and there was tenseness in both. The nervousness of people waiting to fly and the hurry of lateness and anxiety from pas-

192

sengers and employees wanting to get airplanes into the air before the weather closed down and grounded them.

Packard moved across the lobby, his right hand in his overcoat pocket, on the gun. He closed his senses against all images but Farrel's, against any voice but his. He walked among porters bending with the weight of suitcases, among men and women scurrying across the lobby like small animals, past counters and concessions and saw none of them in detail. He walked with the weight of his body concentrated forward on his feet, ready.

When he came to the outbound waiting room and looked through into it, he saw the end of a line of passengers filing out the door to a waiting plane, but he did not see Farrel. He went on again. He came back to the waiting room finally and paused until a group of passengers approached the guard, hurrying, with oustretched tickets. He stepped in front of them and walked through the door.

"One moment!" the guard called.

"I'll be right back," Packard said and went on.

The guard took a step after him and stopped because the late passengers were shoving their tickets at him.

Packard crossed the room, looking, between tables, past a counter on his right, a restaurant concession on his left, toward the door.

A girl in the blue uniform of a stewardess stood by the open exit, checking the names of passengers off a list as the last ones filed past her. A man, also in a blue uniform, waited just outside the door to guide them to a plane when they were assembled. The passengers stood around him like school children around their teacher on an outing, impatient.

Packard squinted to study another group of passengers stringing along behind its guide, moving fast, in a frank walking race for the preferred window seats of an airplane parked away to the right, a hundred yards from the terminal. When he first noticed them through the snow, the front runners were just emerging from a deep space of shadows beyond the floodlighted brightness around the airport buildings, fifty yards out.

He waited until the whole group of sixty or seventy had come out of those shadows and piled up around one another in the lights at the foot of the steps. They were thrusting boarding cards at their attendant and crowding and scrambling, by ones and twos, up the stairs and in through the blue and white side of the Pan American DC-6. And Roger Farrel was not one of them.

Packard relaxed, disappointed, and curiously conscious

193

that he had been staring very hard at the group, expecting something from it. Now he was aware again of the slow, heavy throb in his chest. He moved his head and saw that a stewardess at the door nearest him had lowered her clipboard with its passenger list and was inspecting him closely. She wore the pale blue tailored suit that was the Pan American Airways uniform.

He smiled at her and she smiled back out of politeness and quickly began to study her list again. She had stopped the point of her pen near the bottom of the paper and she looked up once more immediately, across the room, frowning.

Packard looked over his shoulder. Farrel was not there, and the guard at the door had apparently forgotten him. He looked out through the windows again at the Pan American 6, questioning the thinking that had brought him here. Half of the passengers had already climbed into the plane.

Beyond the window, the appearance of a baggage tractor with one following trailer caught his eye. It hurried across the parking ramp, the snow falling in straight glowing diagonal lines through its yellow headlights; like tracer bullets. It turned half left and headed toward the DC-6.

The stewardess finally wheeled around and lifted a telephone out of a wall bracket and began to talk into it.

Far out, beyond the shadows, the line crew and attendants stamped and moved and waited for the Pan American plane to depart, and only a couple of dozen passengers who were not so hurried, remained to be loaded. They knew the good seats were gone. Somewhere to the left, Packard heard the two engines of another plane fire and come alive one after the other.

The baggage tractor and its trailer came to the edge of the floodlighted area and began to be immersed into the darkness between the buildings and plane; the yellow headlights probed weakly ahead. They reflected on the windshield, then picked up the round red bulk of a gasoline truck left squatting in the shadows; moved across it, went past.

And Packard, watching, sucked in his breath and took a long step so suddenly to the right, where the stewardess stood at the exit again, that the pain forced a cough and he stood still for an instant with the sweat starting.

He had seen it, the man's figure, facing toward the DC-6 beside the gasoline truck, surprised by the edge of the yellow headlights, jumping back into deep shadow.

It was not possible with the eye to identify the figure at that distance in the snow and shadow and weak light; but only possible to tell that it was hiding and afraid of being seen; that it had waited there in the cold dark, beside a gasoline truck, out of the warm light of a waiting room; that it had chosen to be hidden until the last moments before the Pan Am 6 left the ground. So that it would not be seen in the building lights. So that it would not be found if someone thought as Packard thought and searched the plane. So that it would not be held up in the light of the boarding steps by crowding passengers.

Packard pointed past his chest with his right hand and said to the stewardess who looked alarmed, "Where does that plane go?"

"To Zurich, sir. Are you on that flight?"

He made a move to pass her. She stopped him by lowering the clipboard from her chest so that it was between them horizontally, against his side. He drew back suddenly.

"What is your name please, sir?"

Packard looked down toward the sheet of paper. There was a pencil scrawl below the blue mimeographed list of names.

If it was Farrel out there in the shadows waiting to ride the Zurich plane, he had to have a ticket. To get a ticket he had to show a passport. And his name went down on a passenger list. If he bought that ticket very late his name would be written, not mimeographed.

"Farrel," Packard said.

The girl jabbed her pen angrily through the pencil scrawl. For an instant she forgot her nice airline manners.

"The whole airplane is waiting for you, Mr. Farrel," she said. "I have just called the office that you are a no-show. Now they will be paging you. Why have you only just stood there?"

"May I go now?" Packard asked. "Before I miss the plane?"

The girl remembered her company behavior. "You will need this, sir." She pulled an oblong of green cardboard from below the clipboard and gave it to Packard. "It is your boarding card. I will show you to the airplane."

"That isn't necessary," Packard was sweating heavily and his body was chilling in the cold wind from the door.

"It is a rule," the stewardess said stubbornly.

Packard looked beyond her. The last dozen passengers were moving up to the steps of the loading ramp at the DC-6. He brushed the clipboard up with his right forearm.

"Look," he said. "You call on the telephone and tell someone not to worry about me. And I can find the airplane alone." He pushed her lightly away. "It's been done before."

Farrel had gotten by this same door; pointing at someone

195

else's name on a printed list probably; taking someone else's boarding card.

The girl moved back from him, staring at his face, reaching behind her for the wall telephone. Packard leaned with his right shoulder against the glass door and opened it wide and went out into the snow.

27

HE WANTED to run, and a fast trotting shuffle was the best he could make of it. He wanted to breathe deep, and an unsatisfying breath of wet cold air that scraped raw into his wounded chest was all that he could get. The cold sweat evaporated on his forehead and under his clothing and he leaned farther to ease the pain and kept going.

He was three quarters across the floodlighted area when the loudspeakers rasped and spoke out harshly—"Will the following passengers report immediately to the Pan American Ticket Counter or go directly to Gate 2 of the outbound waiting room: Ehli; Farrel; Gardiner! This is the final call for Pan American World Airways flight 610 to Frankfurt and Zurich!" The voice repeated in German and Dutch. The click of the switch that shut off the microphone came sharp through the air.

The stewardess hadn't gotten her call through in time, and anybody on the airport who cared knew now where Farrel intended to be and what he was planning. Sometimes, even when the plans and execution were good, you didn't get the breaks.

Packard was close to the edge of the field shadows. This close, the light from the buildings behind him spilled past and he saw the black form of the gas truck unclear but unmistakable, thirty yards away, facing him.

He squinted, with his eyes narrowed against the falling snow, and looked toward where the wheels of the truck should be so that he might see Farrel's feet first, under the body of the truck, silhouetted by the rays from the plane's boarding lights. He could see nothing, and he took the gun out of his pocket and pulled the hammer back and looked up, toward the plane itself, to make sure that Farrel had not begun the last-minute dash for the plane or come out of the shadows.

A man stood under the nose of the ship with a headset on and looked up at the two pilots in their lighted cockpit. Another man in white overalls lounged against his fire extinguisher under number three engine, watching the baggage

196

tractor back awkwardly away from the belly of the plane and jackknife its trailer behind it. The last four passengers were on the stairs of the ramp, and the attendant who had guided them was climbing behind them to the platform at the top with his head bent, a clipboard in his hand, and a stewardess was waiting for him.

Packard had begun a circle to the left as he entered the shadows; so that he could come on the truck in back of the man if he was hiding behind it and facing the plane; so that if he had been seen coming he would change the position of himself as a target.

Inside the shadows the world was not black as it appeared from the waiting room, but only dull and dim. He had come around so that the airplane and its crew were visible to the left of the gasoline truck instead of to the right. They were visible to the left and so, at that instant, was the fat figure of Farrel, unmistakable now in its rolling motion, moving away from the truck toward the airplane, starting to run, and fifteen yards away.

Packard tried to match the run. He took four steps, five, and it was too much. He slowed abruptly to his shuffle, off balance forward, and took in a deep breath to yell. He staggered and bent as the breath brought a racking cough and finally he came up against the rounded back of the gas truck, leaning hard against it, and he lifted up the short, light gun to fire at Farrel, steadying his wrist against the stinging cold metal of the tank. The smell of gasoline was thick around him, and he lined the wedge of the front sight through the rear trough against the black outline figure of Farrel growing smaller. He thought of what the flash might do to the gas.

To hell with it, he said aloud because he could not see a choice, and began to squeeze his hand. Until over the gun he watched Farrel throw up his arms to balance as he stopped short on the slick snow surface of the cement. The baggage tractor had turned sharply under the tail of the airplane, its yellow lights glowing, and headed in their direction. Farrel took four ungainly tentative steps to the rear until he was certain that the tractor was coming directly at him. Then he spun and bolted back for the shelter of the gas truck in unreasonable panic.

Three feet away and in the gloom his eyes lit on Packard. He turned his head to look over his shoulder and see where the baggage tractor was. And then the fact that his eyes had seen Packard registered on his brain and his head snapped back around and he tried to stop and reach out for the gun at the same time.

Packard lurched back and Farrel slammed into the truck

197

with both hands, holding himself upright, finally, by a valve screw and a length of hose, staring at Packard.

Packard lifted the muzzle of the gun and pointed it into Farrel's face.

"Come behind the truck!" he ordered. To speak was an effort.

Farrel's first concern was with his hands. He took one from the steel of the valve screw that must have felt oily and one from the hose that he appeared to have found grimy. He looked at them and seemed to ponder rubbing them on his overcoat, then decided to hold them open, straight down at his sides and well away from himself. He took a step closer, not looking at Packard but at each hand in turn. He had acquired a Homburg hat somewhere and wet snow was piling up on the black felt in gray patches.

"Where is she, Farrel?"

"Where is who?" Farrel looked away from his hands and watched Packard closely. And now he could even make his voice sound bored. "And will you put that up, please, Mr. Gray? Or down?" He indicated the gun by raising his open right hand an inch or two above his waist. Packard saw the fat of his face contract as he wrinkled his nose. "This air is filled with gasoline fumes. The flame from that could destroy us both and you know it. You won't use it. So put it away before there is an accident."

Packard saw Farrel watching his face and his slumped posture, bent and leaning for support with the point of his right shoulder on the tank side. Farrel was waiting for him to cave in. Stalling.

"I'm running short on time," Packard said. "If I start to go down, I'll kill you! Where is she?"

Farrel stepped sideways away from the truck. He looked back at the plane deliberately.

"I'm short on time, too," he said reprimandingly, "and in a moment you will have caused me to miss my flight."

The side glow from the yellow tractor lights came under the truck with the long black shadows from the rear wheels. The small motor clattered close and faded. Farrel stood fixed until it had passed.

"I can't stand here and talk," he said. "It's much too late. If you kill me you won't know where she is. And no one else can tell you. No one that you can find. You don't want to kill anyone. You aren't being rational, Gray."

These were the things that were giving Farrel his self-control and his courage. He knew where Sarah was and that Packard was close to sinking. That a shot could explode the gas truck; and what reasonable man would risk that? His reasoning was only wrong on the last point.

Packard shivered with a sudden chill. The melting snow ran along his ears and face and under his collar. He did not know himself yet whether he would shoot Farrel or not. First there was Sarah to find. And his government was not through with Farrel. Killing would only be a satisfaction for himself.

"No," he said to Farrel. "I won't know where she is. But you'll be dead and we'll have that anyway."

It was turning to words. An open-air forum. It was going wrong and time was short. Farrel knew what he had in his favor, and Packard knew the limitations of a gun and that little talk came out of a dead man. Farrel was not sure enough to walk away. Packard wanted too much from him to fire.

"You——!" Packard shouted, with sudden temper that would quickly drain him but gave him also sudden strength. The word was filthy. "Enough of you! I can do more with a gun than kill with it! Worse than kill you with it!"

He lowered the muzzle. Farrel still held his puffy hands, pale in the shadows, fastidiously wide of his dapper body; open so that they would not even touch their own flesh while it was dirty. He followed the slow drop of the gun with his eyes.

"Don't be silly, Gray," he said. But his voice was rising and it was no longer bored.

A low, slow whine began in back of Farrel and increased in pitch and speed. An engine coughed. There was a dull backfire explosion. Then it caught and settled to a rough idle.

"You're making me miss it! It's leaving me!" Farrel shouted. But he did not turn his head away from the gun toward the plane.

"Do you know where I am aiming?" Packard raised his voice. Another engine had backfired, failed to take hold, and the pitch of its starting whine was rising again. It was getting hard to hear.

"It won't kill you," Packard said loudly. "It will make a hell of a mess of you and you'd be better dead. But you won't be! Where is Sarah, Farrel?"

Farrel stood with his neck bent hard down, staring at the immaculate light front of his overcoat, a thin neat cover over his prized masculinity.

"Think about it, Farrel! They can't patch you! Where is my girl, Farrel? You'd better hurry. When I go, you go!"

Farrel looked up into Packard's face. He had opened his mouth loosely, trying to get moisture into it. A third engine had fired. The shouting had drained Packard so that he was trembling through his whole body; the shouting and the anger and the driving need to hurry had drained him. And he felt

199

the warm, itching trickle of blood coming under his bandage. He began to squeeze his whole hand on the gun, like squeezing a lemon, wanting to fire and to damage, wanting Farrel to yell.

"Here it comes, Farrel! It's going to hurt!"

Farrel looked at the gun; down toward his body; back to the gun. With horror and with disgust on his face.

"Wait!" He shouted. The fourth engine caught, raced, settled to steady.

"I can't wait. Sarah didn't wait!"

Farrel stared, fixed and desperate, once more at Packard's face.

"She's on a boat!"

It was a screamed confessional.

"Ah." Packard kept his aim. He let his hand relax. "What boat?"

"A Polish boat. The *Wilejka*. It left Amsterdam at one-thirty. Stop aiming at me there now!"

Packard raised the gun barrel and Farrel let his hands fall loose against him and his head dropped. He stood limp and sagging; torn open; a pose of abject hopelessness; or shame.

"Where does the boat go?" Packard moved closer because he had to hear and because, for the moment, Farrel was no danger.

"Back to Poland."

A man's voice shouting a short comment passed by on the other side of the gasoline truck. A girl replied, briefly, her voice thin in the noise and muffling snow. They were going back toward the buildings. Packard ran his left hand across the wetness of his face and was not aware of the additional pain of using that arm. His sickness was almost beyond pain now.

"Come on!" he ordered Farrel.

Farrel looked up.

"Such a method!" he said a little wildly. "That you thought of such a method!"

"Nobody on your side would have!" Packard answered, as small boys used to say, So's your old man, because with the anger running out he knew he would have done it even to Farrel with shame. "Hurry up!"

He held his left elbow close in against his wound and gripped his own right arm with the fingers of the left hand to steady the gun. He let Farrel get almost past him, then he decided if anything went wrong with him he wanted one answer before it happened, and he stopped Farrel.

"What made her get on that boat?"

200

"I did, of course. I made her get on it. She thought she was saving you!"

Packard was able to see Farrel smiling at him and waiting hungrily for his reaction. His reaction was relief, above the fear he felt, and beyond what he felt for Farrel.

"Okay," he said, "shove off!"

"You won't see her again!" Farrel shouted.

And the area around them flared suddenly into searing, explosive blue-white brightness. The two of them still stood in the tapered blackness of the truck shadow, stretching two hundred yards to the side of a hangar. But on all sides the shadow area was gone and the blazing light flooded the parking ramp back to the airport buildings. The pilot of the 6 had turned on his landing lights to taxi. Farrel blinked once, shocked, like a mole thrown onto a summer beach, but continued to stare into Packard's face. The snow on his Homburg by now was a white cover.

"You won't see her!" He repeated it. "I took care of that, too! The boat was in the North Sea at four-thirty. She's beyond you now! If you approach that ship they'll throw her over!"

Packard felt the body of the truck rock slightly from a weight on the far side. He felt the door slam and he heard it. He pushed himself away from the tank and Farrel leapt back from his movement.

"You even did me a favor by coming first!" Farrel taunted. "Suppose the Party had come first. Suppose they knew I was leaving! It was just a matter of time. I even thank you, Gray!"

"Stay close to me!" Packard ordered. "You have a message to send! I'm going to use you!"

"That isn't possible!"

"I'll get you to a radio!"

"I don't control the boat!" he yelled. "Even if I chose to!"

"You'll choose to!"

The gasoline truck rumbled, switched on dull headlights that were visible only in its own front shadows. It moved off, making room for the plane to taxi, and Packard and Farrel stood in a world of paining, flooding brilliance. Farrel, shorn of protective cover, jerked his head in every direction; closed his eyes tightly; turned his back on the plane; took a waddling step.

"I place myself in your custody!" he said premptorily to Packard. "Take me out of this light!"

Packard shuffled behind him.

"I'll take care of you. Slow down, Farrel! Don't run!"

The strength was gone from Packard's voice. Obviously gone.

Farrel glanced back without stopping, slyly, to make sure Packard was still behind him with the gun, upright.

"Slow down!"

Packard could hear the plane not far behind them, its engines ticking over; making a slow turn, he judged from the swinging landing lights; waiting for them to get well clear. It was not possible for him to hurry. Nearly impossible to move at all. He might just not make it. Come this close and then not make it. He forced his eyes and mind to focus on Farrel.

Come on, goading himself. You can cry in the morning.

He halted, drunkenly wary, because Farrel had stopped so abruptly in front of him that his shoes left two straight black skid paths in the thin white snow surface. Farrel had his head forward on a stiff neck, like a dog at point, and his hands thrust out straight behind him and open like a racing swimmer ready to dive. Packard raised his eyes and looked in the direction of Farrel's point.

Jeff Funston was standing outside the waiting-room door in the lights of the building and the plane, looking at them. When Farrel stopped and Packard stopped behind him, Funston began to come toward them.

Farrel looked over his shoulder at Packard, then back at the Negro. He took a step backward.

"Get going!" Packard told him.

Farrel backed another step. He pointed at Funston.

"What is he doing here?" he shouted.

"He's your friend. Ask him. Get going!"

Farrel moved another half step back and Packard automatically raised the gun slowly and with great effort, to threaten him.

"Ah!" Farrel yelled. "He followed me too! They did suspect me! It's your duty to protect me! The Party sent him! The damned girl didn't make it! I'm in American custody, Gray! I'm an American. It's your duty!"

He was screaming.

"Here he comes!"

"Shut up!" Packard said. "What are you playing? Get the hell going!"

But it was clear to Packard that he wasn't playing. His face and voice were wild. His little eyes were wide with fear. He had turned sideways with his arms still behind him, edging toward Packard, staring at Funston. Behind Funston, people were coming out of the buildings.

"He's from the Party!" Farrel yelled. "I knew it. I knew it. They had him watching me! I'm your prisoner, Gray!"

"I'm his prisoner!" he shouted crazily at Funston. Funston broke into a loose trot.

202

Farrel searched Packard's face with terrified eyes and reached out a hand toward him in a helpless gesture. Packard's reflexes made him shove the gun at Farrel's face. Packard's vision was beginning to twirl with vertigo.

Suddenly, Farrel whimpered. He twisted his body and tried to run. His feet slipped and he stumbled into Packard, knocking him to the ground. Farrel scrambled for footing and looked over his shoulder and began to run headlong, his arms flailing, his fat legs flying out sideways like a woman's. Packard lay crumpled with his left cheek against the concrete in the snow, trying to bring the gun up and aim it, and he could not. He heard Funston bellow as he went past him:

"Look out, Farrel! Wait up!"

Farrel turned his head at the voice and saw the Negro behind him. He jerked around again and stumbled, off balance. The blaze of the plane's landing lights was shining through the turning propellers, making them look like solid translucent disks.

The form of a disk was suddenly broken by the black silhouette of Farrel's body, outlined sharply. The blades of number one's propeller caught him through the face and head, into the shoulder, and lifted him, spun him around, threw him. The blades of number two came around, down, and cut him down to the concrete, rolling him, until the force was spent and he lay crumpled under the nose of the plane, in the gray side reflection of the landing lights. If he had screamed, Packard had not heard it.

Jeff Funston went around the propellers and reached the body as the people in front of the waiting room began to run toward them in a black bobbing group. He leaned over the body. Then he came back and leaned down over Packard, while the group went running past them.

He covered Packard's gun hand with his own hand, and took the gun and got it into his pocket. Packard, fighting for consciousness, felt it, and he felt Jeff lift his head up and hold it.

"How are you?" the Negro asked him.

Packard shook his head. "No good. This is as far as I go for now. Jeff, I'm sorry about Farrel. I tried to save him for you. But he went crazy when he saw you. He thought you were after him when he saw you. From the Party. Where's your natural cover?"

He tried to make it a joke, but his voice and his smile petered out.

"They won't get him now," Funston said. "He's safe now. Come on. I'll get you off the ground."

Packard pushed against him weakly. People were begin-

203

ning to stand around them, but ineffectively, not wanting to approach. The noise of the engines was dying out.

"Wait a minute," Packard said. "Sarah's on a Polish boat with a name like Weeleshka. Farrel said it went into the North Sea at four-thirty. Will you tell someone, Jeff?"

"I'll tell 'em. Can you believe him?"

"I had him frightened," he said, "but now we can't use him. That will lose her."

Jeff put his arm under Packard's right arm, across his back, and his left hand under Packard's legs and he stood up, lifting Packard into his arms, like a child.

"Jeff, if someone tries to stop the boat, they'll throw her over."

"I'll tell some people."

He swung around gently and moved ahead slowly and steadily, letting people move out of his way. Packard felt the jolting of the steps as Jeff began to walk on. He heard Bob Sande's voice, rough and challenging the Negro. He heard the final silence from the plane's motors.

"It's all right, Mr. Sande." Jeff's voice was deep and natural and quiet. "I'm a friend of his. Will you drive for us?"

"That's right," Packard mumbled. "He's a friend."

Packard's eyes were closed. "Jeff?"

"Yes, Packard."

"He thought you were a Communist."

"That's all right."

"Jeff."

"Yes."

"You were right. Farrel tricked her to the boat."

The Negro understood what he meant.

"Yes," he said softly. "That's fine, Packard. Just fine."

Then Packard heard the thudding feet and the puffing before he heard the voice. They stopped.

"We are told that the man was a close witness," the voice said. Packard opened his eyes to see two policemen and let them fall closed again. "He cannot be taken away until we have had time for questions."

"For Christ's great merciful sake, look at him!" Sande said.

"He needs to be in a hospital first," Funston said.

"Nevertheless . . ." the same policeman began.

"But I am going to take him to the American Embassy," Funston said. "He is an American and wants to go there. He cannot answer your questions now, anyway."

"He must go with us."

"If he goes with you, he will be a dead American on your hands, sir," Funston said.

204

The two policemen talked in Dutch.

"Who is he?" the other voice asked.

"I don't know, sir. But it will be easy to find him at the Embassy."

"Who are you?"

"My name is Funston, sir."

"And yours?"

"Mine is Sande. I write stories for an American newspaper, the *Herald Tribune*. I will be writin' about this one. About the details. About the delays and those kinds of things. I was about to drive this man to the American Embassy. Is that goin' to be all right with you?"

In a very great distance, Packard heard further talk in Dutch. Then—

"You may leave, but we will follow to see that you go where you say you will. Come this way."

They began to move.

"My car is sittin' in the front lot," Sande said.

"We will feel much safer with you behind us, sir," Funston said.

But there was too much pain in Packard for him to smile at Funston's defensive sarcasm. He made a face that was meant to tell Funston to be quiet and not slow them up.

"It's all right now, Packard," Funston said to him. "It's all right. You just hold on tight inside now."

28

THE ROOM was big and square, its walls wainscoted with dark grained wood. Above the wood ran a soft cream wallpaper with small figures in silver. There was a large fireplace, cleaned and empty, faced with white marble, and two deep maroon leather easy chairs at each end of a low mahogany table and a maroon leather couch and a flat-topped table. Heavy blue draperies hung from ceiling to floor, drawn across the two windows. The room was big and square and rich and with the lights on it had the luxurious, masculine feel of a library in a British country house.

Packard lay back under the covers against the clean white sheets with his eyes half closed, staring at the ornate ceiling. The doctor had come and was an hour gone and he was drowsy from an injection. He was on the edge of sleep and deeply comfortable in his release from pain, but he struggled to keep from thinking of Sarah. Because when he thought of her his mind tumbled out of control and his flesh burned with sudden heat and his breath was short and painful and

205

inadequate. Each time he came so close to sleep that his hold on consciousness relaxed, thoughts of her came in on him. So he was lying there with his eyes heavy when the white door was opened and Jeff Funston's face looked around at him and saw his eyes open and smiled.

"Hey," the Negro said. "You still awake? How do you feel?"

"Come on in, Jeff. What's the story?"

Funston closed the door behind him. He bent his body forward and leaned his arms on the thick square top of the dark wooden post at the foot of the bed.

"They're downstairs now, making it up," he said. "They got the Ambassador on his way out. He's down there in a dinner jacket. They got the press secretary on his way to something. He looks like he got dressed in a record hurry. David is down there. Dickson too, hanging around looking like he wants to help, but he's not in good favor."

"It works that way. It's the bird who sent him over this morning they ought to isolate. What about the *Wilejka*, Jeff?"

The Negro studied the pattern of the colored quilt.

"Farrel told it right," he said. "They left Amsterdam at one-thirty. It went up the North Sea Canal and cleared out of Ijmuiden a little after four-thirty. By the time I got you here and called David, they were twenty miles out into the North Sea."

"What time was that?"

"Around six-thirty.

"Now it's eight forty-five," Jeff added, not looking up.

"I know. Jeff, has anyone looked beside the canal?"

"The Dutch did. Their police searched it. She wasn't there."

"The weather's pretty bad. They might miss something."

"Yeah, but it is only fifteen or so miles up there by car from Amsterdam. The country is open."

Packard closed his eyes and let his breath out and began to breathe normally. He hadn't wanted to ask the question.

"Well, they didn't get the letter anyway," he said. "They would have left her where she wasn't hard to find and we could get the blame for killing her."

He opened his eyes.

"Then they can still have her alive, Jeff! You know!"

The Negro's face filled with an ancient sadness and understanding of suffering as he looked up.

"They may have, Packard," he said. "They may still have, but she's gone from you."

"She's out there on a boat, isn't she? What are they doing about it downstairs?"

206

Packard's tongue had been thick with the sedative. Now his eyes were wide open and his voice was weak, but clear. Funston leaned away from the bedpost and put his hands in his pockets.

"They're getting news stories ready. How she was kidnaped by the Russians. That's all."

"For Christ's sake! They'll kill her. The Reds won't let that kind of evidence live."

Packard raised his head from the pillow.

"You lay back," Funston said. "The doctor says you came pretty close."

Packard wadded the two pillows high under him impatiently and put his head back.

"What the hell is the Ambassador thinking of?"

"It isn't the Ambassador, Packard. It's David. And he's the chief of the OSA mission here. Calm down now."

"David!"

Packard said it with hatred in him that the man would interfere. In his assignment. With Sarah. Taking over.

"The Ambassador said no one was going to kidnap an American citizen from him. He wanted to get out patrol boats and have the Dutch or Danes or Norwegians intercept the *Wilejka.*"

Packard said nothing, waiting for the rest.

"David heard him out. Then he said he didn't think it was a very good plan."

Packard had his eyes fixed on the Negro.

"Did he give a reason? Or he just doesn't care for plans?"

"David said let her go."

"Let her go!"

Jeff nodded his head.

"If Farrel had to kidnap her," David said, "the Russians can't use her, and it appears they didn't get the letter. Now they won't claim she asked for asylum because they can't let anyone question her to prove it. And she won't work for them after this. So she can't hurt us."

"But they can kill her!"

Jeff reached beside him with one hand and turned a round-backed leather armchair so that it faced Packard and sat down in it. He put his arms along the wooden arms of the chair so that his hands hung limply over the ends. He looked down at his feet.

"David said let her go. The story of Farrel's confessing to the Party kidnaping a well-known American out of Holland will hurt the Russians all over. Bad. I told him what Farrel said about throwing her overboard. So he told the Ambassador that if we went out to stop her and anything happened, the Americans would get the blame for trying to take her away by force. And if he asked our friends to stop the *Wilejka* with gunboats in international waters and they went aboard and didn't find her, he'd have an incident on his hands."

"This little bird David is all business, isn't he?"

"He looks soft, but he's pretty hard."

"Sure. He's safe."

"Well, it isn't his girl, Packard. It's a job to him. What would you be like?"

"She's his girl, too. She's an American, isn't she? Who the hell does he work for?"

He sat up in the bed, driven suddenly. The pain hit him and the left side of his face twisted up in an open-mouthed shock and he rolled back onto one elbow, panting.

"The Russians can't use her," he said fiercely. "So we will! She's no Communist! I know that! She was stupid. She came awake too late. But they had to drag her off, didn't they? Now she's stuffed on a Pole boat by a lousy traitor on her way to Russia in God knows what shape. And we have a fine plan! We're going to leave her there! She has a big name and the world knows who she is and we can use her for propaganda by just leaving her go. Oh, it's a fine plan."

His voice dropped at the end. The Negro got up and stepped to the bed and pushed him back flat against his pillows with worried gentleness. Packard was shaking and his eyes blurred with tears. He pulled the sleeve of the blue pajamas they had put on him across his eyes.

"Isn't it a fine plan, Jeff? She's out there on that tub alone. Scared dry. And if she ever doubted which side she's on, she knows now. I want her back because I'm in love with her and she's in love with me!"

He lay silent with Jeff's big hand on his shoulder, taking charge of himself. He swallowed hard and then he spoke and his voice was bitter, but he had control again.

"I want her back because I love her, Jeff. And I don't want Farrel to win anything. Even now. And I want her back because if we'll let even one American go like that, alone and frightened and in trouble, so that we can use it, then I won't ever give a damn again which side wins."

Jeff leaned over and pulled the colored quilt back over Packard's chest.

"You love her, Packard," he said. "But David isn't all wrong. It could make a lot of trouble to interfere."

"And the Ambassador buys that?"

"He doesn't like the idea of the kidnaping. But he doesn't want any incidents. He finally agreed. He said after all she got herself into it."

"The hell she did! Well, I don't buy it!"

"You better say these things to David and the Ambassador."

"I will."

"All right. I'll go and get them for you."

"No. Wait."

He put his hands over Jeff's, still on the quilt. He looked absently at the scrolls and flowers and the four smiling faces of cupid on each corner of the ceiling, thinking.

"There's a man down there who doesn't want any trouble and isn't authorized to have any," he said quietly. "And one who sees his chance to strike a blow for our side, which he is expected to do. And I'm here with an assignment from Washington. All we'll get will be arguments and finally cables to Washington for a policy decision. By that time it won't make any difference. I'd better think of something. Then I'll tell them about it."

"You can't do anything from here, Packard. And you surely can't get up."

"Maybe not. Wait around a minute, Jeff."

Jeff sat down softly in his chair. There was a distant scramble of voices somewhere in the building and the fast clacking of a typewriter, in irregular bursts. A car passed in the street beyond the curtained windows, its tires crunching on packed snow. And the heavy sound of Packard's breathing in the room.

Finally he said, sharply, "What did Farrel look like, Jeff—after the propellers?"

"He didn't look like much. He ran in head first."

"How hard would it be to identify him?"

"Mighty hard. Impossible for a time. His face was gone. His body was cut up. And I got this."

Jeff took the long alligator skin wallet out of his inside pocket and laid it on the bed. Packard picked it up with his right hand and glanced at it. Farrel's passport was in its place in a back pocket of the leather. The remainder of his airline ticket was loose in the center fold. Packard handed it back.

"I took it hoping he might have been careless with some names or phone numbers," Jeff said. "I don't know what else he had on him. It was going to get crowded there. There was nothing else in the same pocket."

"He probably didn't get any mail here. What did Farrel do, Jeff?"

"At home? He ran a pay station."

"Long?"

"The FBI has been on him a couple of years. He's probably been at it since the war."

"Big?"

"About ten thousand dollars a month. The Russians put the money in Swiss and Dutch banks. Mostly Dutch. He transferred it across on his publishing house and paid it out to the political-action people for front groups and Communist trials and the like. He also paid off espionage people with it and gave cover jobs to agents inside his business. So the Russians got big money transferred into America legally without a fuss, and they kept their spooks out of contact with their Embassy."

"Then he knew a lot of their people?"

"He was a big shot. The Bureau was on to fifteen or twenty leads just by watching him.

"We all hoped for a lot more," he added sadly.

"That's fine," Packard said. "It's just right. Is Sande still around here?"

"Sure. He's down in the lobby, talking to the marine guard. Waiting for his big story."

Packard was excited. He had a thin smile on his lips.

"Well, bring him up here, Jeff. I'll give it to him."

The Negro sat up straight in his chair, frowning at Packard.

"You can't talk to any newspaper people. Do you forget where you work?"

"I'll remember. Don't tell me not to stick my neck out, Jeff!"

Jeff pushed to his feet.

"All right, Packard. But you've got no authority and no clearance to talk. They can get you under the Espionage Acts. Be sure."

He turned and crossed the room with his long balanced strides. Packard lay with his head on the pillows, going over his thoughts. He pushed the pillows against the back of the bed and, ignoring pain, propped himself up against the pillows and the headboard in a half-sitting position and began to listen for Sande and Funston to come up the stone steps and along the hall.

29

Sande looked around the room as he walked across it.

"Boy," he said. "I wish I had your influence."

"Anybody can get it," Packard said. "If he's the President."

"Or has enough holes in his belly. How are you?"

"The doctor didn't say. He just grunted. Sit down, Robert. Thanks for the taxi service."

"A pleasure."

Sande started to sit down in Jeff's chair. He looked up at the Negro standing at the foot of the bed.

"Was this yours, Mr. Funston?"

"Sit down."

Sande shook his head.

"No. You take it. I'll think faster on my feet in front of the schoolteacher here anyway. What do you know, Packard? Mr. Funston says you're in a talkin' mood."

"Bob, if I give you a story and you give it to Robertson and Doornbos, how soon will it come out?"

Sande looked curiously at Packard.

"Why if I was to share it, which I won't, and it was a stop-press kind of item, it'd be around the streets here by early mornin'. At home, too, with the time change. But I'm not a wire service."

"I want you to share this one, Bob, or I won't tell it. And it's got to come out fast."

"Suppose you just tell it to me, Packard, and let's see."

Packard smiled at the stubborn look on Sande's wide face.

"All right," he said. "You'd better take notes. It has to be right."

"I don't ordinarily use notes in interviews."

"Well, use some this time, will you?"

Sande finally sat down in the chair, spreading his overcoat apart.

"Ready?"

"Fire away."

"Item number one," Packard said.

"Sarah Borsen," he recited, "escaped as a stowaway today on a Polish ship, the *Wilejka.*"

Sande raised his head sharply. Jeff looked at Packard, his forehead creased in a deep frown. Packard went on.

"Although she had no permits from the American Department of State to travel and no authorization from the Polish Government, Miss Borsen appears to have stowed aboard the *Wilejka* without the assistance or knowledge of its crew as it was preparing to sail from Amsterdam today."

Sande finished writing.

"It that straight fact, Packard?"

"Sure it is."

"Who said it?"

"An official spokesman for the American Embassy in The Hague who does not want to be named."

"Are you an official spokesman?"

"Right now I am. You can fill in whatever background you want as long as that part goes."

"What about Farrel? And that other big boy who walked out of the hotel with her?"

"Item number two," Packard said. "The American publisher, Roger N. Farrel, was taken to the American Embassy in a state of shock this afternoon after managing to knock a gun from the hand of an unknown assailant who threatened him when he was preparing to depart aboard a Pan American plane from Schiphol Airport."

"What are you givin' me, Packard!"

"Just write it down, Bob."

"In attempting to escape, the assailant fled and apparently stumbled and fell into the turning propellers of the aircraft and was killed instantly. Mr. Farrel was taken immediately to the Embassy of his country by another American for medical attention. There has been no statement so far, although the police are investigating."

Packard lay back against the headboard.

"And anything else you want to put in?" he asked.

"How about fillin' it in with a little of the truth?"

Sande was suspicious and annoyed.

"I can't send that stuff out, Packard. I like my job. It feeds me. What's this baloney all about?"

"You made me a speech last night," Packard said, "about keeping Sarah from the Russians. Well, we've got a few thin hours to get her back from them and we've got a plan. These stories can make or break it. We might not get her anyway, but if you get them splashed around in a hurry, we just might."

"Is this for the government?"

"It won't hurt them either. But it's for me. I want her back. For myself. And for her."

"I'd better talk with the Ambassador or one of those people fussin' about downstairs, Packard."

"If you do, you ruin it. I work for Washington, too. And that's for your ears only. But I'm asking a lot so you have a right to know. Or you don't have any right, but this might help you think my way."

Sande looked up at the Negro, leaning on the bedpost again, watching Packard.

"I figured," he said. "What about this, Funston?"

"I don't know what he has in mind," Jeff said. "So far I don't see any harm to anyone but him. And a lot of work for the police."

Packard saw Sande smile as if it pleased him that it made work for the police. He stood up and stuffed the notes into his overcoat pocket.

"I'd better just give it to Tommy," he said. "I can talk to

212

him. I don't know about Doornbos; he might want to check it here first."

Sande put his hands in his coat pockets. He stood looking at Packard with his big shoulders hunched forward.

"Okay," he said. "I close my eyes, boy. I'll send it off. Not for you, mind. I'm thinkin' of the pretty Miss Borsen."

"So am I. Thanks, Robert. When the whole story comes out, I'll see that you get it first, if I can. If you get in any trouble, I'll see what I can do. Get it out fast, will you?"

"Sure. I'll phone it around. Someday I'd like the story on you, too."

"When I'm up, we'll have a drink."

"Okay, you can buy."

Sande said, "So long, Mr. Funston."

He walked across the room and opened the door.

"You don't mind if I change your writin' some? It might help you get her back. And I don't mind bein' fired, but I resent bein' disgraced."

"Shove it," Packard said. And Sande waved his arm and pulled the door shut after him.

Jeff Funston shook his head.

"You're wild, Packard," he said. "Who's that going to fool?"

"Lots of people, I hope. They'll all get it straight in a day or two, but with the weather and different people talking and Sande's stories, it will take a while; and I'm counting on the confusion. Nobody saw it all the way through. Nobody even saw most of it. And after tomorrow, it won't matter. Now you can do something, Jeff."

The Negro frowned.

"I hoped I might stay out of it," he said. "I don't want to go where they're going to put you."

"Just an errand. You'll stay out of it. Most of it. Got a pencil?"

"Yeah."

"Did you ever hear the Party boys call Farrel anything but that?"

"They called him a lot of things. They said he was a right-deviationist and his publishing business was run bad, and he was living too high . . ."

Packard started to speak.

"I know what you mean," Jeff said. "They called him Alex when they were up in his room. They all called each other by Party pseudos. I guess it's a good idea. I didn't get any names. We might try it."

"Okay. Then write this down. It's a radiogram. To the *Wilejka*." Packard dictated slowly: "ROGER N. FARREL

213

CALLED ALEX IS IN MY CUSTODY. HE HAS TOLD ME THE
NAME OF YOUR SHIP AND WHAT YOU ARE CARRYING. IF YOUR
CARGO IS PUT ASHORE SAFELY ANYWHERE IN HOLLAND SO
THAT IT REACHES THE AMERICAN EMBASSY HERE BY 1100
HOURS TOMORROW, FRIDAY, I WILL RETURN ALEX TO HIS
HOTEL WITHOUT FURTHER QUESTION AND YOU CAN HAVE HIM.
IF WE HAVE NOT RECEIVED YOUR SHIPMENT I WILL DISCLOSE
HIS WORK HERE AND HE WILL BE FLOWN TO AMERICA FOR
FULL INTERROGATION AND WE WILL INFORM THE WAY YOU
LOADED YOUR CARGO AND LODGE FORMAL AND PUBLIC COM-
PLAINTS. And sign my name to it," Packard said. "Farrel's
already handed in my name. I won't be any good in this
neighborhood for a few years anyway."

The Negro stood looking at the paper in his hand.

"I don't know," he said. "I don't know."

"You don't know because you know Farrel is dead. It's
a chance I take. The Party might know it, too."

"You think they'll send this?"

"You stay there until they do. Have the clerk put it into
Dutch for you; or, better, German, if he can."

"If you're going so far," Jeff said, still looking at the
message, "why not sign the Ambassador's name? That
would give it more weight."

He was sarcastic.

"Then they wouldn't send it if you came in with it. And
I want the Comrades to think I'm pulling a private dirty on
the government. I think they'll believe in that kind of a
doublecross where they wouldn't trust an official offer."

Jeff folded the paper and put it in his coat pocket. He
leaned away from the bed.

"Farrel's name was on the passenger lists, probably," he
said. "They have part of his ticket. They can't tell anything
from looking at him, but his name is all around."

"They have a name and they have a body and they can't
tell who the body is, and I'm telling them, through the
newspapers, where the name is. Farrel, they'll read, is alive
and in the American Embassy. Farrel made this mess for
his own good. I'm glad to use him to get her back, if I
can. Okay?"

Funston shook his head again.

"Pretty good," he said, "if you are lucky. You've got it
all figured out except what Nick is going to say about your
acting like God or a private citizen. Which you aren't. Why
don't you talk it over with them, downstairs, first, Packard?
I don't like doing it this way."

Packard stretched himself out full length again on the
bed. He flattened the pillows under his head.

"Nick is a friend first. And then I have an assignment,

214

from Nick: Keep Sarah from going to Russia. Do it as an individual. Keep the U.S. out of it. Nobody has changed my orders. I'm doing it the way I see it."

Packard pulled the quilt up over his body. Funston was frowning.

"Let me explain it through, Jeff, and see if you can find any holes in it," Packard said.

The Negro waited, looking down at the bedpost.

"The newspapers will say that Sarah stowed aboard the *Wilejka* on her own," Packard said, "which will save face for the captain. He can put her down somewhere and not worry about trouble with the police. His alternative is to be charged with kidnaping, get in trouble at home for bungling, and not be allowed in any Western port again. I count on his not liking that.

"It saves face for the Reds. They can order the *Wilejka* back and be sure the Americans won't claim publicly that Sarah was kidnaped. Because an American Embassy official has already told the papers that the Poles had nothing to do with it. I haven't hurt us, Jeff. It will only be harder to use her for propaganda."

Packard closed his eyes and spoke slowly. "The Russians can't use her. David is right. They ought to be glad to be rid of her, to keep it out of the papers. When the ship gets my message, they will probably stand by where they are and radio back here, and maybe to Poland, for orders. If you were the Reds, would you rather have Farrel or Sarah?"

"Farrel, if I could get him."

"When they get the radiogram, they'll think they can have him. Their people here will call the police, who will say they have no information. Farrel had no luggage at the airport. You have his papers in his wallet."

Packard opened his eyes.

"You'd better not carry that around," he said.

"I'll put it somewhere. Don't you worry about it."

"That's fine. Then they'll call the papers. If they don't, they can read them on the street at six or seven in the morning. Farrel, they will find out, is in the American Embassy and hasn't made a statement yet. Someone they will have to guess about is dead at the airport. Have I hurt us so far?"

"No, I guess not. But you know it's out of line and . . ."

"Now if they believe what I want them to, and what they'll want to believe, the Party will think I got to Farrel and that I want Sarah back enough to make a deal. He tells me where she is. I get her back and let him go. I'm not giving them time for any staff studies or policy reviews, or orders from Moscow."

215

"They might have time."

"They might! They might a lot of things! But Farrel is a big wheel. He's passed their money. He knows about their projects at home. And he knows a lot of their people. If they order the *Wilejka* back with Sarah, I let go of Farrel. If I let Farrel go, they grab him. They protect their operations and agent nets at the cost of a girl they don't want now, anyway. What would you do, Jeff?"

"Why, I suppose I'd trade. But I'd want to see Farrel first."

"They don't have that choice. They can't contact me. It's natural I'd be here with Farrel—and out of their way after last night. Have I hurt us?"

"It doesn't seem so."

"Then get the cable off, will you?"

The Negro pulled the paper out of his pocket again and looked at it. He rolled the fingernails of his left hand on the square top of the bedpost. "I guess this is your case," he said finally. "You have a right to give the orders."

"If there is any blame, it won't hit you, Jeff."

Funston looked embarrassed. "I'll take a cab outside to some cable office," he said.

"Thanks, Jeff. And when it's done, go on back to your room in the L'Europe and wait. Farrel's friends will come there looking for you, if the cable works."

"Okay."

"Tell them Farrel phoned from the airport and asked you to bring him something out of his room—his passport. You were there when all of this happened, and you brought Farrel back to the Embassy because he asked you to. Tell them that when you left, I was alone with Farrel and no one else was allowed in the room. And you'd better have a story for the time between when you left here and when you got back to the hotel. Talking to you might clinch it for them. If you've seen Farrel alive and me alive, which ought to be their most serious doubt, it will sound pretty good. Be careful with them, Jeff. Don't go out with them."

Funston said, "I'm not stupid, Packard. I just don't have as many friends as you have—or better have."

"I'd give myself the same advice, Jeff. You'll have the part that takes guts. A lot can go wrong. They might know she's dead. Or Farrel's dead. They might decide not to deal. They might be afraid of a trap from you. I might get twenty years. But this is all I can do, and I've got to do it. I want her back that much, and I don't want them to have her that much. A man does what he can and what he has to. Then he's earned the right anyway to wait and hope. You go on.

216

I'll hope. I'll hope for Sarah. I'll hope she didn't grow up too late."

"I'll pray a little for her on my way to the cable office," the Negro said.

Packard raised his eyes and looked at him closely.

Jeff's face was serious, and his voice was low and gentle.

"Good," Packard said. "It might help if you do it. Thanks for everything, Jeff."

The Negro turned and walked to the door and opened it. "Jeff."

Funston turned his head.

"When you go by ask David and the Ambassador to come up here. Tell them it's urgent.

"Don't stop and talk with them," he added.

"Sure."

"By the time they get here you'll be gone. If the thing is already done, I guess they'll help with it, not having a choice."

Packard rolled his head on the pillow.

"We always have to wait to work together until it has already happened," he said.

"Yeah," Jeff said. "It seems so."

He closed the door behind him. Packard listened to his footsteps along the hall and down the stairs. He looked up at the ceiling and began to think of Sarah. He thought of her in her trench coat and he turned his head to see if they had put her perfume bottle with his other things on the table beside the bed. It wasn't there and he looked up again and closed his mind to her as a girl that he loved and began going over his plan again, looking for errors, testing it for traps.

After a while he heard a door slam below him and heard the grinding start of the car across the snow, out of the drive; he closed his eyes and shifted his weight, to the right, away from the pain, and lay back to wait for David and the Ambassador. And hope for Sarah.